Eyes on the Pryze

Eyes on the Pryze

Felisha Bradshaw

www.delphineepublications.com

Published by Delphine Publications, LLC

Publishers Notes

This book is a work of fiction. Names, characters, places, and incidents are either products of the author's imagination or are used fictitiously. Any resemblance to actual events or locales or persons, living or dead, is entirely coincidental.

Copyright© 2010 Felisha Bradshaw

ISBN: 978-0-9821455-4-8

All rights reserved including the right of reproduction in whole or in part in any form. Without limiting the rights of the copyright reserved above, no part of this publication may be reproduced, stored in or introduced into a retrieval system, or transmitted, in any form, or by any means (electronic, mechanical, photocopying, recording, or otherwise), without the prior written permission of both the copyright owner and the above publisher of this book; except in the case of brief quotations embodied in critical articles or reviews.

Lyrics from "Warning" Copyright © 1993 by Christopher Wallace and "Gimme the Loot" Copyright © 1993 by Christopher Wallace. Ready to Die released on Bad Boy Records 1994

www.delphinepublications.com

DEDICATION to Rudolph "Rudy" Sneed

In Memory of:

James Bradshaw(Father), Shaahyid Mathews, Maurice&Andrew Dickson and "Rocky" from Oasis Market, Tremaine "Fats" Newsome, Andre Moore, Ean Flemming, Martin Moore, Irene Bradshaw(Grandmother) Louella Cousins(Aunt Lou) may God take your worries and replace them with wings.

Acknowledgments

Through God all things are possible. We all have unique gifts from the creator; our Father and my gift is writing. Thank you father God for my blessings. I will use it to my fullest capability.

With that said, I'd like to thank the love of my life; Chainelle Caban. A shout out of faith to my children; Jamaira Watson and Jaylyn Bradshaw, Marnell Lomax(Step-son) and Tameka King (Step-daughter). See you guys God had my back and he can have yours if u let him. To my mother, doing it again...so much better the second time around. To my brother; James Bradshaw and sister; Michelle Bradshaw Ellis, I love u guys enough for the both of us. Give my nieces and nephews hugs and kisses. Got send a spiritual kiss and a hug to my Pastor, Derek Calhoun and wife, Lady Sharron. Thank you, New Vision International Ministries, for giving me a place to worship where I feel nothing but love and an anointing in the air. It is our season and definitely a time for transformation and restoration. <u>Bishop Vaughn M. McLaughlin</u> at Potter House House Christian Fellowship, We all love you at NVIM. Momma Gee, you're the best, hey, Cassandra Bentley, Terrance Crawford, Kee-Kee, and all my other NVIM members.

Thanks for the support to my favorite cuzn; Wyateisa Hanley, (Hey Sunshine!) and a slew of cuzns. What's up Black? (Allison Sloan). Thanks for the on going support; My aunts and uncles, Lois Gainer, Kim White (Lady Scorpio), Dorris Wheeler from The Biz, Aurora Jones from Leznation Media, and a handful of my favorite people and BFFs; Juanita Johnson-Davis, Rashida and Darlene Joyner, Nyniia and LaLa Bishop, Honey and PopPop, Hope Johnson, Tye, Shannie, Henry Shissler, BAYM home of the $77 computers, love you Elliot. Charles Nixon (Chuck), Mashie, Chris "ifudon'tmentionmeI'llkillu" Weaver, Tia Speed, Princess Dawson, Tishana Davis, Kim Swinton, Craig Waddell(CJ) keep your head up, Noemi and Macho, Tessy Samuels, Karen; I'm on my grind! Taura Rogers, Tracey

Pugh, and Lucinda Moore, Rochelle&Keith Henderson, Thanks, Quaylyn Caban for grindin' for me. Thanks, author SIDI for putting my book on 125th. Hey Theresa and Andre Caban. Take care of my godchild, Iris Valesquez. I Love U man: William Chapman. Hey people, get the Darkest Gray, by V Lyric Parker it's a must read. Marie Poole we should be due a long conversation after this...lol. Debbie Pettway we will be friends until the end of time. Charli Domelevo, I have to send love to her. Where are u? Hit me up on Facebook. Keep supporting us Black Book Clubs; Sistah Candice of The SistahFriend Book Club, AAMBC, Alice Holman of RAWSISTAZ, Cheryl H. of APOOO Book Club, Real Divas of Literature; Lady Scorpio. Last but never the least the woman who grinds hard for her passion; literature, my publisher, Boss Lady and a true diva, Tamika Newhouse. U can check us out on www.Delphinepublications.com along with Anna Black; author of Luck of the Draw.

For anyone that I missed, I apologize. Be blessed and stay encouraged

CHASE PRYZE

People always wondered why my mother named me Chase. I was too embarrassed to tell them that my moms did it as a joke. See, my pops was forever 'chasing' that high. Her, too. Both of my parents were junkies. That 'caine will do it to you every time. Growing up with junkie parents was like having no parents at all. So, I took to the first thing that showed me love ... the streets.

I earned much respect in the streets for my swagger. I fought anytime somebody tried me. That's how I got this scar on my cheek. Cha! That's just how it goes when you grow up in the hood. And nobody got your back.

Supposedly, I got a twin brother ... somewhere. That same day I got this scar, I really could've used a brother, then. Me and him would've been kicking ass all over Washington Heights. Side-by-side. So, I finally worked up the nerve to ask my moms about him. She told me, 'just be lucky I got your ass back. One child's enough to get me a welfare check. Ain't no telling what happened to his ass. Now shut the fuck up and let me get this high.' So, I ain't never ask about him again. At least one of us made it out, though, y'know?

It's just me and these streets. Feel me? And when it comes to these streets, I'm king! Niggahs need to know this!

WHICH WAY DID HE GO

"That niggah is gonna pay!" Chase Pryze sat in his Mercedes Benz contemplating his next move. He slammed his fist on the dashboard as he looked out at part of his empire that was forever keeping him rich. Stratford Avenue, aka: The Ave, was the spot for any addict to get what they needed. Chase's 357 Crew held the entire Ave, a few local bars, and two local housing projects: P.T. Barnum and Charles Greene Homes, on lock. Nothing went down on those streets without Chase's doings or knowings.

Half-Black American and half-Jamaican Chase stood six-four; slender but firm build. The scar on his right cheek gave him a renegade look. That, and the dreads that rested on his backside meeting his waist. The Colombian men who hung outside the bodega, down the street from his building, loved that he didn't take no shit.

"Papi chulo, ven aquí. Joo wanna make some money?"

Chase jumped at the opportunity. He began as a runner: a messenger boy, and that evolved to selling packs. Then he became their number one transporter. As he grew older, he became their connection between suppliers.

Chase never knew his father kept tabs on him, and was hip to what he was doing. How could he not be? After all, Chase never asked his parents for anything, always kept his dreads well-groomed, and always wore a fresh pair of Air Force Ones.

Eyes on the Pryze

His normal drop-off was scheduled for that evening. His father followed him to one of the spots to do a pickup. He passed his father in the stairwell. Holding tightly to the handle on the duffel bag, Chase went over his boss's instructions in his head: drop the money, pick up the drugs, and bounce. Easy as pie, like always. He never thought twice about his father's presence.

Chase skipped up the stairs and checked the area with two quick glances before knocking on the steel door in the usual code: three pounds and a tap. Eyes of coal peered through a small cutout in the door. Chase raised the duffel bag to show he was prepared for the exchange. His father unexpectedly approached him; asking questions, clouding Chase's judgment. Out of nowhere, five gunmen rushed up the steps. Before Chase could make a break, one of the men grabbed him and pushed him to the bottom of the stairs. Shots rang out.

"Run, bwoy! Go to your yard!" Chase's father shouted.

Antonio Velez, Chase's Colombian boss's only son, had been inside the apartment chucking bricks of coke into another duffel bag. He ran out the door when he heard the ruckus and was caught in the midst of all the gunfire. Chase's boss blamed him for his son's fate. So, at the tender age of thirteen, Chase Pryze became a wanted man.

Chase kept the money the Colombians gave him to make the buy, left New York, and started his own empire. On his way to the train station, Chase ran into an old head named Cutty who knew Chase's father in Kingston. Cutty took Chase under his wing and brought him to Bridgeport, Connecticut. Chase did not tell Cutty that he had enough money on him to take care of himself. At this point in the game, young Chase knew he could trust no one.

Felisha Bradshaw

He worked for Cutty on the block where Cutty served as lieutenant. Chase, a fast learner, watched how business ran and decided that he'd soon have his own block. He stayed with Cutty and one of his many women in the Charles Greene Homes. Five months later, Cutty's crib was raided. Cutty had just enough time to flush a few bricks of coke down the toilet. This left Cutty owing his boss for the loss. Because Cutty never asked young Chase for anything and cared for him as a son, Chase told him he had enough to cover his debt. From that moment, Cutty became Chase's protector and mentor, and dedicated his life to his friend's son.

The next thing they did was set up shop on The Ave. A corner turned into blocks...blocks turned into territory. The Notorious Chase Pryze and the 357 Crew developed from there.

Now twenty-two, Chase treasured everything he'd acquired through the game. He wasn't about to let Rajii's robbing him jeopardize his empire, and take what he'd built!

GET DOWN OR LAY DOWN

"Cutty?" Chased rolled down his window and signaled his right-hand man to come to the car.

"Wha'um bredren?"

Cutty, a true Jamaican, wore his dreads in a kufi and kept at spliff burning at all times. He's lived in the States over twenty-nine years, yet refused to give up his heritage and become what his father used to call Americans ... Yankees. He was like Robin Hood to the neighborhood kids, but they knew not to cross him. If anyone ever, death would be the only solution. Cutty opened the passenger side of Chase's car and slumped down in the seat.

"What's up with Rajii? I haven't seen him in two days."

Rajii, one of Chase's lieutenants, collected earnings from The Ave and oversaw some of the runners in the crew under Cutty's command.

"Mi check pon 'im since den, 'im gone! Mi jus sen de likkle youth, Wayne, to check 'im yard, but nuttin come up." Cutty knew Rajii was never going to turn up.

"Send a message to his mother," Chase grabbed Cutty's arm. "Don't kill 'er, but mek she know mi wan what is mine," he made his point in affected Jamaican patois. "There's a snake in the grass and I want his head cut off!"

Cutty knew what Chase meant, and exited the car.

Felisha Bradshaw

Chase's cell phone rang. It was his girl, Phoenix. She was the exception to the rule: money over bitches. Chase loved her innocence.

"Chase, I need you to come to the house. My girl, Vina, needs to talk to you about something," her voice was sexy even when she talked business.

"What's up? She always has something to talk about!"

Vina, aka: V, was a gossiping chic, but Chase cared about her as if she was part of Phoenix's family. She grew on him, being Phoenix's best friend.

"I don't know what it's about. Just come check me." Phoenix respected the game. She knew what could be said over the phone.

Phoenix sat on the edge of her bed confused. For the first time, Vina wouldn't tell her what gossip she was holding. This worried Phoenix. Vina couldn't hold water, but was leaving her girl thirsty. Shit must be serious.

"Vina, I called Chase like you wanted. He's on his way here now. You coming?" Phoenix asked, eager to know what Vina had to say.

"Call me when he gets there. I'm smoking."

Vina contemplated how best to tell Chase about Rajii. She didn't want to tell Chase she was seeing one of his enemies, especially Blizz. When it came down to a man's crew eating, coming between rival ballers wasn't the thing to do. But Chase has been her girl's man for what seemed like forever. This niggah, Blizz, however, has only been up on Vina a few weeks.

RAJII

There comes a time when a young man has to step up to the plate and choose sides. Now was Rajii's time. He was given an ultimatum...either get down or lay down. Rajii sat in his RX7 staring at 357's earnings. Get down or lay down? Shit! It's time to get down. A niggah's gotta eat. He stuffed the duffel bag under the seat and headed to the North End to meet his new boss.

Rajii was a young head looking to step up his game. His new boss's team had what it took to reign supreme. Not only did his new boss hold the Terrace on lock, but he was expanding; taking little crews in the west and south ends as well as Marina Village and Marina Apartments, a local housing project, and making them part of his team. Blizz promised Rajii territory where he would get ten G's weekly. Rajii knew it was his time to shine. When he was down with Chase, all he got was a few G's.

See, Chase, you should've gave me that opportunity to be your right-hand man. I told you I was ready.

Rajii pulled into the first parking lot in what used to be known to him as enemy territory—the Terrace, a low income housing community. Rajii checked his watch. He was on time, but where was his connect? Where's Blizz? He suppose to be here. Rajii didn't feel safe waiting there. Too many muthafuckahs out this piece. I don't see how they eat. Rajii pulled Nina from his waist and laid ol' girl on his lap. Feeling at ease, he popped in his favorite CD to keep him alert.

gimme the loot, gimme the loot

Rajii smiled. Biggie Smalls was the man. He told stories of Rajii's youth.

Just then, a tap at the window startled Rajii. A glock stared in his face.

"Yo, son, you snooze you lose!" Blizz laughed as he put his metal away.

"That shit ain't funny, man. You was about to catch fire in that ass!" Rajii removed his hands from over Nina, "I never sleep."

Rajii grabbed the duffel bag that held 357's money from under his seat, handing it over to Blizz; minus thirty percent. Rajii nodded and pulled off. No turning back now.

CUTTY

"Chase nevah learn!" Cutty hissed his teeth, "Too much trust, nevah enough respect."

Cutty continuously called Rajii's cell and sent 911-6 to Rajii's pager. He knew this would turn out a no-win situation. Cutty knew the news he had to report to Chase would hurt him to his heart. He didn't even bother to trouble Rajii's mother because instinct told him Rajii was long gone. He pulled into Mama's Patties on Boston Avenue located just a mile or so from Rajii's betrayal.

"Lemme git two patties wit cocoa bread and a Stout."

Cutty walked out the restaurant and sat on the hood of his car, flipped open his phone, and served Chase with something that would tie his stomach in knots. "Bredren, mi find out wha' gwan wit de likkle youth. Mi check pon 'im. Call 'im wit de code, but 'e nevah answer. So check dis, when yuh gimme de word, 'im dead."

Cutty listened to Chase's instructions then closed his phone. He walked back inside Mama's Patties to retrieve his lunch.

Rajii pulled up to the red light directly across from where Cutty parked. He spotted Cutty's car in his usual lunch spot. Instant fear dripped from his brow. He turned his sounds low and sped through the light.

Cutty exited the restaurant seconds too late. The hairs on the back of his neck stood at attention. This always told him an enemy was near. Cutty headed back to the block, as Chase instructed, though his instincts told him otherwise. He didn't understand why Chase didn't want to get down to business; finding Rajii before the trail leading to him became impossible to trace.

CHASE

"Mi cyan believe dis shit! Rajii de same likkle 'omeless fuckah mi bring outtah de dirt! Mi fed 'is bitch ass, and dis wha' 'e do to de 'and dat kept 'im eatin?"

Chase sat in his two-bedroom stash house on Sixth Street, known as Six Block, just off Stratford Avenue, thinking about the day he met Rajii; thinking about Rajii's first attempt to get down. And I respected that niggah's gangsta.

Rajii was thirteen-years-old when Chase ran into him going into Pettway's Variety, on the corner of Fifth and Stratford, to buy a loaf of bread. Pettway took pity on him and slipped in some lunch meat and cheese. Rajii looked in the bag and placed the meat and cheese on the counter.

"Anything I get, I work hard for."

The memory brought a smile to Chase's face, still couldn't believe Rajii had betrayed him. But an example had to be set, so his other workers would know crossing him was akin to digging their own graves. With all this chaos going on, Chase forgot to run by Phoenix's house to find out what Vina wanted to tell him.

"First things first."

Talk to Cutty, set a plan in motion to catch Rajii. Time was ticking away. He knew all Rajii's hangouts, and time was not to be wasted.

Felisha Bradshaw

Chase called out, "Cutty!" Voice command on his cell phone automatically dialed Cutty's cell. "Call Mike from 357. Ask him to give his old girl at the DMV a call. See if she can run Rajii's plates and give us the 411 on who registered his car. Then you can take it from there. You know what to do. One."

Chase couldn't believe what he just did. Rajii was like a little brother to him. Street fam was all he had, but there were no exceptions. Rajii had it coming. Chase sat back, refocused on some financial matters. He took a great loss. But like any other major baller, he had stacks set aside for rainy days, like today. What was he to do? His family had to eat.

PHOENIX

"Where is he?" Phoenix repeatedly dialed Chase's cell. "Something must be wrong. Since when hasn't he answered my calls?"

Phoenix plopped down on her queen-size bed still holding the book that she couldn't put down all day. As she turned the page of Tiffany Wright's Fallen Divas, she heard a car pull up. She jumped up hoping to see Chase. "Damn! I should've known. It's that new cat she's been seeing. Maybe this one will last." Phoenix turned her light off so Vina couldn't see her spying. She made a mental note to talk to Vina about her new friend. "Not bad. Go, V!" Phoenix left the window, giggling to herself.

She turned the light back on and continued reading her book. After reading a few more chapters, she decided to take a long shower—just in case her baby wanted to love her when he arrived.

VINA

Vina's parents died in a car crash returning home from a New Year's Eve dance, eight months before her eighteenth birthday. Her father was pronounced dead at the scene. Her mother had been thrown from the vehicle, and spent the following three months in a vegetative state. During that time, Vina got up the courage to have the machines disconnected.

No one in Vina's family cared enough to step up to the plate. The remaining months before Vina became a legal adult, her best friend's parents agreed to foster her, so she wouldn't wind up in foster care until her eighteenth birthday. Phoenix and Vina's mothers had also been best friends, so it was like being with family. She loved and respected P's parents for looking out for her.

Once Vina's financial matters were in order, she moved back into her parents' home. Her parents had put a substantial amount of savings away, as well as a separate account for Vina's college education. They also left insurance money. A clause in the insurance policy provided that the policy would pay off the house in full in the event of her parents' simultaneous deaths. The house was Vina's, free and clear. She was also able to collect social security benefits because she was under eighteen when she lost both parents. Vina had no worries, just loneliness; the loneliness she felt each night alone in her parents' house.

Eyes on the Pryze

She filled that void by getting smoked and, occasionally, spending quality time with her new family across the street.

Vina promised herself that no man would shit on her, or what her parents had worked hard for. So most—shit—all her relationships were short, unattached, and solely to fill a void. The few men in her life were mere boytoys. It wasn't hard for Vina to get what she wanted; not with that curvaceous body of hers, and the form-fitting, provocative, yet fashionable, clothes she wore. A natural beauty, Vina inherited her high cheekbones and almond shaped eyes from her Trinidadian mother; her chocolate skin from her Cuban father. She wore her hair in a mohawk. The only makeup she wore was a touch of lipgloss. Not your typical 'round-the-way girl.

She lay on her bed half-naked watching the latest videos, picking up tips for her Saturday night ventures to the Van Dome in New Haven.

"Psst! V! Psst! V!" Blizz hollered up at Vina's window from the front lawn. Vina came to the window and saw Blizz holding up a bag of smoke, pointing to the rear of the house. "Come on, boo!"

Vina motioned to Blizz that she was coming down. *That niggah better be glad he brought me some medicine. He knows he can't break the rules: call before you come or at least be invited. He can't just be popping up at my place.* Vina slipped on her silk robe and met him in the back, unaware that Blizz was setting his plan in motion.

I've been here over five times and no ass. And I gave this chic gifts and took her out. It's about time I get mine.

He was about to bring out the freak in her that went with that banging ass body. He had ready-made blunts hidden in the ziploc bag filled with a half-pound of purple haze.

Vina opened the screen door with a smile on her face. She noticed Blizz in swimming trunks sitting on the edge of the pool in the middle of the backyard.

"Come over here and let daddy give you what you need." Blizz leaned back on the edge of the pool with his feet dangling in the water. He laid a blunt on his tight abs, and Vina smiled devilishly.

"You are too much," Vina looked at his passion rising in his trunks, "and I do mean too much." She wasn't a freak, but there was nothing like a big dick and a bag of smoke. Blizz had both.

Vina picked up the blunt from his stomach with her teeth, and rested her head beside his passion. She sparked her blunt, Blizz sparked his; both unwilling to share. After the first three pulls, Vina truly thought she was on a cloud, and she could fly. Blizz had to stop her numerous times from attempting to jump from the edge of the pool.

"Betcha I can walk from one end of the pool to the other without getting my feet wet."

Mission accomplished.

Blizz called his crew, the Dough Boys, telling them to park around the block and walk to her house. Before Vina attempted her stunt, Blizz grabbed her by the arm and sprawled her out on the lounge chair. She faded in and out. From that moment on, Vina would never remember how she became a porn star, or why she trembled with fear each time she heard the word train.

Blizz reached into his pocket, retrieving his mini camcorder. He removed her robe and, according to plan, she made things very easy for him. She was picture perfect. Her skin glistened under the stars. Blizz knew she would have never consented to unprotected sex, and this was his opportunity to feel her silky insides. He attacked Vina. Vina couldn't gain control of her thoughts or actions. She felt free one minute and restrained the next. There was sunshine, then rain, then the sun shone as it rained. She couldn't distinguish her imagination from reality, so she giggled.

Some of the Dough Boys entered the backyard, and thought their eyes were deceiving them. Ms. 5000 was high as a kite with her legs spread wide open.

Phillie wasn't a member of the Dough Boys and she was the only female present, but you couldn't tell that by the way she carried herself. She's had a sweet tooth for Vina since elementary school. Now seeing Vina giggling in freak mode, Phillie thought she was in the middle of Willie Wonka's Chocolate Factory.

Blizz saw the lust in Phillie's eyes.

"Yo, Phillie, glad you could make it. We've been getting fucked up. Vina said she couldn't wait to have her first experience with a woman, and she wanted you. You just gonna stand there?"

Phillie didn't need to be asked twice. She came prepared. She wore her nine inch strap-on just for occasions like these. None of the Dough Boys objected to Phillie getting first dibs. For them, watching live action between two women was like having your birthday fall on Christmas. Blizz made certain he had a clear shot of Phillie and Vina's interlude. Phillie passionately kissed and licked Vina all over. Vina imagined the man of her dreams was making love to her. She spread her legs and moaned. Just as Vina started becoming lucid, Blizz blew smoke from a laced blunt into her nostrils.

Phillie recognized the scent. Damn, he got her smoking dust and haze! Phillie sensed something about all of this wasn't quite right, but dismissed the thought when Vina opened her mouth for a shotgun.

Vina had tried to speak, but couldn't once she felt the burning sensation at the back of her throat. She thought she was choking and she reached out for help. She felt someone in her grasp but, by then, she danced on clouds again.

Phillie grew excited when Vina pulled her closer. Now was the time for her to put Kong, her strap-on, to work. Phillie moved in and out of Vina, sensuously loving her down, until her body trembled then collapsed. She buried her face in Vina's chest and breathed in her essence.

The crew cheered Phillie on. They wanted an encore. Phillie went on for another hour; until she brought Vina to a place where the ocean waves crashed against the sand. Blizz frowned. Damn! That's like three times this dyke made her cum. Fuck that, a dyke will never get hold of any more of my bitches. Blizz seized control of the situation, telling Phillie he thought Vina had enough. He tapped Rajii on the shoulder. "She's all yours, young Raj."

Rajii was in another realm. He tried to fathom why Vina allowed this to go down. He knew Vina casually, and had never heard anything in the streets about her being a jump-off. She would've never let these raggedy niggahs run up in her like this. But, shit, a niggah's gotta do what his dick tells him.

"Yo, Raj, I said it's on you, my man. Take it as an initiation into the Dough Boys."

Eyes on the Pryze

Without another thought, Rajii put on the condom Blizz handed him while Blizz blew more smoke into Vina's nostrils. Then, one after the other, the Dough Boys went to work on Vina until her legs collapsed.

That unsettling thought revisited Phillie. She looked on in horror and began to see things clearly. This was no consensual sex game. She wanted to put a stop to this horror, this crime, but knew she was outnumbered. Only thing she could do was leave. She reached for her pants, "Yo, Blizz, I'm out. I got shit to do, man."

Blizz laughed and spoke loud enough for everyone to hear. "Nah, Phillie. Ain't nobody leaving here. Everybody's in this shit to the end." He grabbed Phillie's arm and nodded to one of his boys. "Bitch, you ain't really part of the squad. These niggahs here already know. We live by the code. We need to keep your ass here, so you don't get all soft on us and run tell dat."

Phillie continued redressing, trying to hide her fear.

Blizz wasn't taking any chances. "I know how we can make sure this shit stays here." He turned and looked at Phillie, "This is your lucky day." He then looked at the crew. "Phillie's gonna be initiated into the crew. Anybody oppose?"

One after the other the crew brutalized Phillie, as they'd done Vina, until an hour before sunrise. They left them lying on the ground in the backyard.

Phillie was in shock—the first time she'd ever been penetrated. She lay covered in semen staring up at the misty sky as it turned to day. Her body felt lifeless. Her insides raw and bleeding, and a nasty taste in her mouth.

Felisha Bradshaw

Vina's body was worn out. She, too, had semen all over her body as well as her hair. Vina came to and noticed half-filled condoms scattered all over the ground. She wiped her face and looked at her hands and recognized the scent. She didn't recognize the awful taste in her mouth because swallowing was something she refused to do, but figured it out after looking at the pasty film all over her body. Slowly, she sat up with sharp pains shooting throughout her pelvis; her rectum burned.

She tried to recollect what happened to her. She looked at the ground, noticing empty 40-ounce beer bottles, Hennessey bottles, and used condoms all over, she knew no man could have consumed that much liquor and not be passed out beside her. Vina glanced over thinking she would find who she'd slept with. To her surprise, an old schoolmate lay beside her, in worse condition. Not only was Phillie covered in semen, but she reeked of urine. Dried blood matted her pubic hair and stained her mouth. Vina shook Phillie's near lifeless body.

"Girl, you alright? What happened to us? How'd you get here?"

Phillie lay there without saying a word. Vina became frantic, looking around as it dawned on her what happened. Realizing they'd been gang raped, Vina screamed as she sat bringing her knees to her chest then wrapped her arms around herself, saying softly, "Phillie, who did this? Who did this to us? Why?" Tears ran down her face as she looked at Phillie staring into the sky. She slid over to Phillie and tried to snap her out of it. No use. Vina collected what was left of her sanity then went in the house to get a basin of soapy water.

Eyes on the Pryze

While Vina was gone, Phillie took the little strength she had to locate her strap-on and toss it into the bushes. Since Vina obviously couldn't recall what happened to her, Phillie hoped that Vina also wouldn't remember that she, Phillie, wasn't just a victim, but an assailant, too.

Vina returned from the house and slowly began nurturing Phillie back to life. She cleaned her as best as possible. Phillie's guilt of what she'd witnessed worsened with each stroke of Vina's tender touch. After drying her off, Vina helped her put on sweatpants and a wife beater. With gloved hands, Vina cleaned up the backyard, and threw away anything hinting at what happened the night before.

"Phillie, I think you need to see a doctor. We both do. Do you remember anything? I've been trying my best to figure out why I'm even in the backyard, and who I was back here with. I can taste the weed on my breath, but who I smoked it with I don't have a..." At that moment, Vina remembered calling her girl, Phoenix, and asking her to tell Chase to come by. She also remembered Phoenix telling her that he was on his way. "No! It couldn't have been. Nnno! He wouldn't. I wouldn't." Vina dismissed the thought immediately. Chase didn't even get high.

Phillie could tell Vina remembered something. She tried standing up. "Ugh. I, I, I gotta go."

Vina jumped up. "No! Please? Phillie, don't leave. I can't stay here by myself, and I definitely can't tell anyone what happened. I don't even know what I'd say or where to start. Just chill here with me for a few days, at least until I can figure out what happened to us."

This was too good to be true. Phillie wondered if she stayed, could her TLC alter Vina's memories, if or when they came back.

"I, I..." Phillie didn't want to seem too anxious to stay.

"That's that! We'll just act like we're having an on-going slumber party. I never did get to invite you when we were little."

It was final, Phillie was staying.

Vina told Phillie to follow her inside the house, and showed her where she'd be sleeping. The doorbell rang. Vina looked up at the clock on the wall and saw the hands indicating six thirty in the morning.

Who the fuck is this? Maybe it's the same bastards that raped us.

Vina grabbed a bat. She opened the door and, before she could swing, she noticed Chase. Unsure if he was the culprit, Vina stayed on her P's and Q's. When Chase moved closer to her and raised his hands to say what's good, Vina swung the bat. Chase stepped back. Vina dropped the bat and fell into the porch railing. Chase caught her in his arms, just in time, before she fell down the porch steps. "What the fuck's up with you?" Vina balled up and cried. Chase, taken by her tears, knew something was wrong. Vina was a trooper; hard as hell. Chase carried her into the house like a gentleman and laid her on her couch. "Yo, V, what was all that swinging shit about? What's wrong with you?"

Vina heard the sincerity in his voice. Thankful, she knew in her heart it wasn't Chase. She wanted to tell him what she thought, but knew Chase would tell Phoenix. Vina didn't want that, but knew she had to tell Chase something. She wasn't sure if Phillie wanted anyone to know her business, so she told Chase just enough, leaving Phillie out of it. Between sobs, Vina told Chase she awoke in the backyard, raped, and believed there had to be more than one person because of the numerous condoms and empty liquor bottles. She told him that she didn't even remember how she got in the backyard, but came-to with the taste of weed on her breath.

"Get the fuck..." Chase stopped midpoint, realizing what Vina told him must be true. He knew V's relationships didn't work out but, like Rajii, he'd never heard anything in the streets about her being easy or a jump-off. "Think, V. What were you doing last night?" Vina told Chase the last thing she remembered was Phoenix telling her he was on his way. "You, you don't think I had anything to do with this shit?"

Vina confessed, "Nah, Chase...well, I did at first. Then I wasn't sure...then when you raised your hands, I got scared. That's why I swung the bat." Vina began to cry.

Chase, sympathetic to her story, yet felt relieved at the same time.

"Chase, you have to keep this to yourself. If Phoenix finds out, she'll just worry herself to death. She needs to stay focused on graduating from college. You know how she is. She might even tell her parents. They'll definitely make me move back in with them. I don't want them to look at me different. I've been holding it down for a while on my own and, plus, they just told me how proud they were of me...I, I, I don't want to let them down. You gotta give me your word."

Chase knew if he gave her his word he'd have to stand by it. His word was his honor and was always bond...no matter what. Chase tried to convince Vina to see things another way.

"Maybe it would be better to tell Phoenix. If all that happened and no one heard you, what's to stop them from coming back? Huh? Tell me, V, because you don't need to be here all by yourself." Chase paused, hoping V would see things his way. "I mean, I could send a 357 niggah by here every hour but, come on, anything can happen!" Vina's expression didn't change. She wasn't going for it. "Come on, V! I've never kept anything from Phoenix." Chase pleaded with her. Keeping a secret from Phoenix was like lying to her. He knew one lie would lead to another.

"I won't be alone. I took care of that already. Plus, I'm getting a registered piece for this bitch!"

Not much Chase could say to that, so he gave her his word.

PHOENIX

A familiar purr eased Phoenix's fears.

I must be some sort of stalker.... Nah, everyone knows the sound of their man's car when it pulls up. Phoenix rushed to the bathroom to freshen up. Must've been business. Chase would never ignore my calls. Phoenix lit a few candles and lay back on the bed. Ten minutes passed, still no Chase. What the hell is he doing? I don't know how long I can act surprised to see him.

Phoenix peeked out the window again.

"What the fuck!" She couldn't believe her eyes. Vina ... Chase...Phoenix's heart fell to the pit of her stomach while watching the love of her life and her sistah-friend embrace. Vina—in her man's arms—holding on to him for dear life. "Ain't that a bitch! No wonder her ass didn't want a relationship. Why would she need one when she's loving mine?"

Phoenix started to bum-rush their asses, but her intuition told her to play it cool. She told herself maybe she was seeing too much into things. Phoenix's heart, which only skipped a beat for Chase and the sistah-hood she'd developed over the years with Vina, was now stuck on stupid. It took all she had to continue watching life as she knew it pass before her eyes.

Chase carried V into the house.

"No! This can't be happening. Chase would never betray me." Phoenix battled with her emotions. She already began making up any and every excuse to explain away what she witnessed. Maybe he's practicing how he's going to ask me to marry him. He said when his business was solid, I would become Mrs. Pryze. Maybe that's why he took so long to come here...tying up loose ends. Maybe he's asking Vina how to go about asking me...or even showing her my ring this very moment...yeah, that's it. Phoenix wiped away the tears forming in the corners of her eyes. Aaaw, baby, I'm so sorry for thinking the worst. Phoenix gained a new outlook. How can I make it easier for him? Maybe I should set the mood. He gets so caught up in the moment of things.

With newfound hope, Phoenix searched for the CD they played the first time they made love. They were younger, and it was a first for both. They went to the doctor for a full checkup, and to learn the best protection to use to prevent pregnancy. Back then, Phoenix giggled as Chase fumbled around with the condom for fifteen minutes. That damn thing was too small. Who knew then that they came in sizes?

It was Phoenix's senior year, and Chase was taking her to her prom; although her mother disliked Chase for being a high school dropout with addicts for parents. Phoenix remembered how she lied to her mother about Chase working two jobs just to pay for his tuxedo and their limousine. Not to mention her three dozen roses: a pink dozen, a red dozen, and a white dozen; representing the three years they'd been together. That was the first time she ever lied to her mother; they had such a close relationship. But Phoenix knew she could never share with her mother that he was a drug lord. Her mother wouldn't understand how her daughter could love a young man who fed poison to the community.

Over the years, Phoenix's mom and dad grew to love Chase as their son. Chase made sure Phoenix went to school. He wanted her to become something, fulfill her dreams. When Phoenix applied for college, Chase offered to pay her tuition. Through this offer, Chase gained her father's love and respect. Phoenix's father realized that Chase wasn't stealing his daughter from him, but helping her evolve into a young woman bound for college.

Prom night their young love escalated to intimacy.

Phoenix realized an hour had passed, reminiscing. She finally found the CD, popped it into her stereo system, and paused it at their song. Phoenix began singing.

My heart is filled with so much love

hmm, hmmm, hmm, hmmm, hmm, hmmm

"Surface was the shit!"

She waited by her bay window. Chase exited Vina's home tugging the waist of his jeans. He reached in his back pocket and retrieved his handkerchief, wiping his forehead then his mouth. He walked to his car, hopped in, and pulled off. Phoenix couldn't believe her eyes. He wasn't coming to sweep her off her feet? He wasn't coming to ask for her hand in marriage? He was leaving.

Phoenix ran to the phone and dialed Chase's cell.

"Yo, what's good, ma? How's daddy's baby?"

Phoenix, taken aback by Chase's nonchalance, yelled, "where are you, Chase?"

He stumbled over his words, "Uh, I'm on the other side of town. I had something to do right quick."

"Something more important than me! I've been calling you all day! You couldn't stop by here to see me?" Phoenix couldn't hold back her anger.

"Boo, I'm sorry. What? You miss daddy? I ain't have a chance to stop by that side of town all day. I couldn't stop doing what I was doing at the time."

Phoenix grew enraged. She couldn't believe what she was hearing. Tears fell from her eyes; each teardrop lessening the love she felt for Chase and Vina. Why would he lie about being at Vina's? Fucking bastard!

"You know what, Chase Pryze? Fuck you! It's over!" she slammed the phone promising she'd never pick it up again to call his ass.

Phoenix then picked up the phone to block all of his and Vina's numbers. She refused to even speak his name. Phoenix had a nice sum of money saved from what Chase constantly gave her. But he spoiled her, never giving her a chance to spend it. So, she decided she would transfer to NYU at the end of the semester. When she applied for college, NYU was her first choice—until she fell so deep in love with his ass. She chose instead to stay close to home, close to him.

To hell with them. Fuck 'em!

Phoenix blew out her candles then cried until the wee hours of the night. Her last tear would be the last time she'd cry for lost love.

CHASE

I can't believe I gave my word. Chase looked up at Phoenix's bedroom window. He nervously adjusted his pants. He knew she'd called him all day yesterday; promised himself he'd make it up to her later that day. Just knowing he was holding a secret from her caused beads of sweat to form along his top lip. *Shit! A dead giveaway. My baby will know something's up.* Chase smiled, realizing how close they'd grown over the years. His business was doing fine up until the incident with Rajii. *What the fuck is up with Cutty? I haven't heard from him all night.* Once matters at hand were out the way, he would take Phoenix on a much needed getaway.

The idea gave Chase some time to avoid Phoenix, at least until he touched base with Cutty. Chase jumped in his car and sped away. He had a few things to take care of. Chase knew Cutty was out looking for Rajii, so the block needed tending to. The vibration of his phone against his hip brought Chase out of thought.

"Yo, what's good, ma?" He knew she'd question him for not calling her back, but damn! *Did she just say it was over? I know she didn't just give me my walking papers. Cha! My boo's such a drama queen...spoiled ass.* Time was ticking, but Chase chose to let her calm down and come to her senses before calling back.

Felisha Bradshaw

Chase stopped to check on his weakest block. These niggahs better step up their game. I need to see what this niggah, Mike, can do to get things right out here. Chase wanted to put Mike in charge of his operation in the Greenes. Mike was a low-key, seasoned beast. Straight out of New York's Douglas Street projects, where they stayed on the grind 24/7. Mike was super paranoid since he was wanted by NYPD for killing an officer. I know this niggah will keep his ear to the pavement and his mind on the grind. This time I won't let this cat know that I'm putting him on until the time is right. I'll just switch up his post from the Ave to here.

Chase pulled into the middle parking lot where he got word that the Yetas, a Puerto Rican gang, had been moving in on his territory in front of building three.

The younger heads ran this spot because it was constantly being raided by 5-O. The younger hustlers were least likely to snitch when they got hit...the penalty was far less for them than those over sixteen-years-old. Most of them went straight to Juvenile and, as long as Chase kept them tight while doing their stint, they were straight. They called it earning stripes for their set.

When Chase pulled in front of the building, he noticed his crew sitting in lounge chairs sipping 40's. I know I told these little niggahs to set up shop, but this ain't a fucking vacation spot. They're truly on some vacation shit! Chase rolled up and jumped out on his lieutenant.

"Yo, Nigel, wha'um say my yout! Whatta gwan wit dis? Tings nah run right, seen?"

Nigel knew when Chase's accent kicked in, he was not a happy man. And when Chase wasn't happy, that made

Eyes on the Pryze

Cutty too happy—trigger happy. Nigel didn't need Cutty's crazy ass on his back.

"Bossman! Nuttin wrong. Tings runnin smooth. Product movin, bredren." Nigel's trembling hands passed Chase a wad of bills. He thought that would save him from Chase's wrath. But Chase had to make an example out of Nigel for his slackness. He backed Nigel into the lobby of the building and pulled out his ratchet knife while the other 357 members looked on. With swiftness, Chase cut Nigel from one ear to the next. Nigel screamed, holding the sides of his face.

"Listen, bwoy, dis nah dibby dibby business. Yuh nevah put mi pon de spot like dat, seen? Yuh cyant gimme money in de eyes of dem. Mistake numba one." Chase kicked Nigel in the stomach with the side of his foot. "Numba two, yuh nevah sleep, seen? Nevah! Yuh outtah luck. Yuh see de earnings from dis spot run low, so yuh carry it." Chase stepped on Nigel's stomach and reached down into his pockets, taking his *PC. "Yuh nah sleep seen two days yuh owe mi. Eedah dat or mi cancel dis."

Nigel chose to work off his debt, knew he messed up. He let his workers get too comfortable with him. He wasn't ready to be canceled—not with three baby mamas. "Yes, mon, mi 'ear yuh."

Chase gave Nigel time to stand. "Get dat taken care of. Mi send Mike to check yuh,"

Chase said, exiting the building. When he reached the front of the building, all the chairs were gone. A mother walked by with three sons. Chase handed Nigel's PC to

---

* *Piece of the Cake*

her. "Take dis...fuh de youts." It never was only about the money.

Nigel walked out of the building in shame. Three-five-seven never forgot the amount of blood that dripped from Nigel's face. They knew the man who left them standing in awe was none other than The Notorious Chase Pryze. They immediately stepped up their game.

Chase made a second run to another of his spots: P.T. Barnum, his goldmine. He had to respect these niggahs' gangsta. This was truly the projects, not a strip like the Terrace. Driveways led to other driveways like a maze. To outsiders, it was a community within a community. There was no way for niggahs to run up in here zooming in and out, busting shots. If anyone tried to run up in here, they'd better be good, or prepared to be bagged. Regardless to who sold drugs for whom, everyone stuck together. Money was to be made in multiples.

Chase pulled up to the courts, where people ranged in age from old-school heads to babies walking topless in Pampers. Everybody knew who he was looking for.

"Yo, Lynx, Dread is looking for you."

Lynx met Chase on the courts.

"What's up, dude? Get in." Chase loved shooting the shit with Lynx. They drove through each spot where Chase had workers while Lynx broke down to him which niggahs were his main grinders.

"Yo, Chase, rumor's out that Rajii's missing with the Ave's earnings. What's up with that young'en? Thought that was your man? That niggah needs dirt sprinkled on him."

Eyes on the Pryze

Chase was not surprised the news spread so fast. He nodded at Lynx. "'im soon dead."

"Where's Cutty? Cause you never make runs out this way. What's hood, G? Things a'ight? You know if you need me..." Lynx tapped his waist letting Chase know he was strapped and ready.

"Everyting's in motion, seen?"

Lynx saw pure rage in Chase's eyes. "Chase, man, you know you can switch that Jamaican accent on and off in a minute," Lynx tried to break the ice—the ice grill that consumed Chase's face.

"When mi breathe, it just comes out." Both laughed and tapped fists then got down to business. "Yo, Lynx, you straight on that? What's the flow like?"

"Mo' money, mo' money, mo' money," Lynx was a jokester, one not to be played with. "Check this..." Lynx instructed Chase to pull up to his girl's building. He ran into her crib. When Lynx returned, he carried three Nike boxes in a clear shopping bag. He always had something for Chase, and he knew how to conduct business. Two boxes contained bundles of hundred dollar bills. The third box held a pair of Jordan 5's. Lynx winked at his boss.

"You know what I like," Chase opened the sneaker boxes. "You know you love that shopping. Good looking. I hope you're keeping a stash and not spending all your dough."

The word dough sparked a memory in Lynx.

"Yo, man, speaking of dough, I heard Rajii was seen with one of them punk ass bitches."

Chase's eyes could spit fire. "Dough, as in Dough Boys?" Chase took a deep breath, "Dat likkle yout is dead, seen?

Felisha Bradshaw

Yo, Lynx, mi soon check yuh." Chase pulled off without another word, not wanting to believe his ears. "I know Rajii didn't betray me twice." The Dough Boys were Chase and 357's number one rivals. Chase flipped his phone and spoke. "Cutty!" Cutty's voice mail answered the call. "Yo, Rajii dealing with the Dough Boys! Check that for me. Call me."

RAJII

Rajii spent the rest of the morning in his apartment, located in the upscale gated community, Avalon Gates. His old girl hooked him on to posing as an out-of-Stater, and renting the apartment over the Internet. He mailed the deposit and the rent, then keys were mailed to him. Just like that. The landlord never knew he was underage.

When Blizz hit him off with ten thousand dollars and the thirty percent he kept from 357's earnings, Rajii laid out his crib. Knowing Cutty would be searching for his RX7, Rajii traded it in for a Cadillac Escalade. For a young head, he was doing big man things. Everything about him was changing, down to his appearance. He was too smart to go back to his mom's raggedy layout to get any of his clothes, so he had to start from scratch. Out with the old jerseys. Rajii now rocked a preppy look. He stopped by Headquarters barbershop and had his braids cut to a low Caesar. He liked his new look; it made him feel and look mature. He went from hood to all good—from Rajii to Shop—knowing that it wasn't in his best interests to use his name in the streets. He chose Shop because that's what he planned on doing...and shopping was all he was about.

gimme the loot, gimme the loot

Rajii looked around his new place and nodded in approval. Now all I need is a sweet ass bitch to keep my shit clean and my dick happy. The thought of keeping his dick

Felisha Bradshaw

happy made him think about the night he ran up in Vina. Damn, V! Rajii rubbed his shaft. I need a freaky ass chick like you. I can't believe Blizz did that shit and taped it, too. Now that shit there would be valuable in the right hands.

Rajii didn't like knowing he could be linked to a sex crime. At the time he knew he had little choice, since it was part of his initiation into the Dough Boys; but Vina was always cool with him. It hit him that in just one week, he'd betrayed the only niggah who gave him the opportunity to eat good. Not only did he diss Chase, but the only people he knew as fam: The 357 Crew. He was the closest one to Chase besides Cutty. Now he knew why Blizz chose him, but he still didn't know Blizz's plan.

Get down or lay down! ...Ten G's a week. It sounded like he had little choice then, but now he questioned his handing over seventy percent of 357's earnings to some niggah he never saw before. Rajii was puzzled why Blizz hadn't made contact with him since he made the drop-off. He knew he was being used, but at a price he thought he was satisfied with. He knew money couldn't be the reason Blizz's boss was after Chase. Everybody knew the Dough Boys were eating just as much as 357, if not more. Rajii decided he couldn't sit and wonder why this and why that, so he put his thoughts aside and jumped in the shower. He was going to find out a little more about the Dough Boys and their boss.

Rajii knew Cutty was out for blood—his blood. And from experience, Rajii knew Cutty wouldn't let up until he was dead. He needed a plan to get rid of Cutty, and soon. Time was not on his side.

First things first...Blizz. After getting dressed, Rajii hopped inside his ride and headed to the Terrace to link up

Eyes on the Pryze

with Blizz. He made a mental note to find a girl who lived where he was going to shit, so Blizz would never know exactly where to find him. Rajii stopped at the gas station on Reservoir Avenue, a few minutes away from the Terrace.

"Let me get a pack of 'ports. Nah, make that a box of Black 'n Mild, and twenty-five on number four."

Rajii walked back to his ride, never taking his eyes off the passing cars. He clicked the handle, allowing the gas to pump itself. He then sat in the front seat of his car with Nina sitting at his side in the open armrest.

"Excuse me?"

Rajii place his hand on Nina then turned to see who was talking to him. Damn! He had to look twice at the beauty who stood before him. A stunning beauty. Rajii never took his hands off Nina, though. He knew bitches were used to catch a man slipping.

"Could you pull up, so I can pull in to get some gas?"

Rajii never been at a loss for words, but this chick had him staring at her without answering her question.

"Uh, uh, pull up? Oh, sorry, ma. No doubt, no doubt."

Rajii got out of the truck and unhooked the pump. He watched her ass switch and glide on air all the way to her hoopty. Damn, I'd like to peel that onion. Rajii gathered his thoughts and got up the nerve to step to her. "Can I get your name, ma?"

"My name? For what?" the girl had attitude.

It didn't matter that Rajii was riding on 22's, or that his grill was worth eleven G's, or that his chain swung when he walked, and landed on his dick when he stood still. Her attitude made Rajii step up his game. He liked that she wasn't your ordinary hood chick. He had to bag her.

"So I can tell the world who my wifey is. That's why!"

She liked his swagger. She couldn't resist his game. This was a first for her.

"What's your name? I don't just give out my government like that."

Rajii was taken by her 'round-the-way girl style. Most girls of her caliber had their heads stuck in the clouds, making it damn near impossible to get at them.

"Ra—Shop. You can call me Shop. Now can I know your name, or should I just call you Beauty?"

She smiled and tilted her head. Yeah, that did it. He knew he had her.

"Well, I guess. It's Jamaira. Now where's my ring? I can't be wifey without a ring."

Rajii pulled his pinky ring off, leaned into the driver's window, and placed it on her finger. "So, it's official."

Jamaira stared at Rajii in disbelief. "I can't take this." She pulled the ring off her finger and handed it back to him.

Rajii stepped back. That ring's worth three G's. "Why not?" Rajii wasn't used to girls giving back; only used to them wanting and taking.

"Why not? This must be worth three, four G's. We just met. Plus, my mother always taught me that nothing in life is free. What am I gonna have to give you?"

Rajii knew this one was a keeper. Before answering her, Rajii thought out his response. He didn't want Jamaira to think that he was trying to trick with her.

Eyes on the Pryze

"Jamaira, all I want is your time. Just think of the ring like this: time is money, right?"

Jamaira's eyes shined when she smiled. "Well, I guess..." she was beginning to like this young man.

"I'll be right back."

Rajii returned inside and purchased a Boost Mobile. When he returned, Jamaira was writing her telephone number on a matchbook.

"Here, ma, this is for you. I want to be able to get my money's worth of your time. When the minutes run out, we're even. Anytime we spend after that will be because you choose to, a'ight?"

She agreed.

Rajii waited for her to open the phone, so he could get the number. He then walked away.

Yeah! A niggah's sweeet! Damn, I'm good!

Rajii headed for the Terrace. Before he pulled into the first parking lot, he flipped open his phone and called Blizz.

"What's hood? I just pulled into the lot. Come check me. I'm ready to get down."

Blizz was impressed with his timing. He hadn't called Rajii. He wanted to see how hungry he was. Rajii's position would be based on his eagerness to get with the Dough Boys.

Rajii placed Nina in the small of his back then got out of the truck. Niggahs were grilling him.

"What you need, partner?" said Diggy, one of the Dough Boys. They didn't recognize him with his new look.

"What's up, Dig?"

Diggy stepped back. "Yo, Raj, what's up with that?"

41

Felisha Bradshaw

Rajii insisted the guys in the crew called him Shop. "That other niggah, Rajii, was 357. He don't exist no more. Shop is straight repping Dough Boys...till death do us part."

This testimonial won the Dough Boys' approval. They thought Shop was gangsta for that. They didn't know they just let a snake into their camp. Blizz appeared. He smirked as he caught the tail end of Shop's brief speech.

Yeah right, bitch. It ain't all good in the hood. Death will soon part us.

In order for Caine's plan to work, Blizz had to keep quiet. He even kept it from his boys, knowing in the end they would understand. When all was done and final, everybody would understand.

"A'ight, y'all, lunch is over. Time to grind." Blizz put his arm over Shop's shoulder and started to walk off.

"Get dough!" The Dough Boys shouted in unison then dispersed.

Damn, these cats are true soldiers. Rajii knew he'd joined a winning team, although concerned about his role in it all.

"Let's get down to business. I want you to be on the lookout for all the teams. Tonight we'll meet at the Ritz Club on East Main. All the knights of the round table will be there. You'll get to know who they are. That will make you an official Dough Boy. But right now, let's get an early dinner so we can discuss it in detail."

CUTTY

Cutty traced Rajii's car to a dealership in Shelton. He hoped that if Rajii bought a new car, he would be stupid enough to keep the same plates so the new car would be easily found. After talking to the dealer, he knew finding Rajii was going to be difficult.

Cutty checked his phone and saw he had a text message. He'd turned the phone off while talking to the girl at the DMV.

Cha, mon! All de while mi dealin wit dis Yankee gal, Chase done got a lead. Cutty jumped in his whip, realizing he couldn't carry things out alone. He needed 357's help—and fast. Cutty called Mad Mike to set up a meeting with his Heavy Hitters. Cutty's team of beasts met at Lennox Cuisine on Boston Avenue, neutral ground for all hustlers. After they broke bread, Cutty explained what he knew so far of Rajii's whereabouts.

"Rajii 'im bright. Chase taught 'im too well. We mus tink like snakes in de grass and walk like chameleons. Dis is de only way we gon find 'im, seen? So, any mon dat tink deh cyan find 'im, Chase gon pay out twenty G's to de man dat catch a teef."

With the stakes that high, it was every man for himself.

***

Vina and Chase both tried contacting Phoenix. She blocked both of their numbers and any of their affiliated numbers from her phone. When they called from other numbers, they were both told she was unavailable or that she just wasn't home. Vina even went over to see her in person, but Phoenix wasn't willing to see her. Chase hadn't gotten much sleep after he tried to call his girl and she refused him; his visits were not even welcome. He was even escorted off her college campus when he tried to meet her at one of her classes. During this time, Vina still had her house guest and their friendship grew stronger by the day. Vina began developing feelings outside of just friendship for Phillie. As for Phoenix, the end of the semester drew near and she'd been accepted at NYU for the next semester. Change was now part of all their lives.

ALONE IN THE BIG CITY

Phoenix settled in. With the amount of things she carried to school, you would've thought she was renting a two-bedroom apartment. Because she was petite and beautiful, she had no problem getting one of the guys hanging around to help her carry belongings to her dorm room. Having wrapped her life around Chase the last few years, she almost forgot what flirting was like. Phoenix reached her dorm room. Her roommate was not there, so she enjoyed the time she had alone. Her father made sure that she had one of the biggest rooms, even with a roommate. He knew his princess wasn't used to sharing her space.

She stood in the window for a while, taking in the scenery. She could see all of the campus from that window, so she chose that side of the room then placed her groceries in the mini fridge. Phoenix then sat on the edge of her futon and all she could think of was him and Vina. I should've at least said goodbye to Vina, Phoenix thought while unpacking. She tried to leave anything linking her to Vina and him, but they'd played such major parts in her life for so long she didn't have anything to decorate her walls. When she unzipped the side pocket of her duffel bag, out fell a picture of him and her. She fell to her knees. Why? I thought what we had was special. I was going to be your wife. Why did you take that away from me? Phoenix drifted to a time and place that made her happy.

Felisha Bradshaw

***

The room glowed with flickering candlelight. Their silhouettes danced on the wall. His hands were large but silky. She could feel them gently touching her soul. His warm, tight muscular frame pressed against her body. She wanted to melt inside him, feel what he felt, coincide with his groans and moans. He fitted inside her comfortably, like it was home. They danced on each other's bodies until they fell into a warm lake. His lips, full and soft, traced the outline of her figure. Her lips followed his lead, returning the favor. Her insides were running faster, rumbling, doing somersaults...faster and faster...until she could take no more. She wanted him to know she knew he was coming home, and that she would soon follow. They met in the same place. She called out his name, "Chase!"

***

Phoenix found herself missing the very thing she was running away from. Tears rolled from her eyes without her permission. She tried to save them from falling by catching them in her hands. She looked up at the entrance of the door, hoping her knight in armor would be standing there waiting to sweep her away. She was about to call his name when someone else stood in her view.

"Hey, mami! I see joo made jorself at home already." As the young girl came closer to Phoenix, she noticed that she was crying. "What's da matter? Joo homesick already?" she sat beside Phoenix. "Hi, I'm Carmen, but my friends call me Cahree." The R's in her words rolled off her tongue like a revving engine; a dead giveaway that she was Spanish of some sort. "I'm jor new roommate."

Phoenix came out of her dream state, "My name's Phoenix. I'm from Bridgeport, Connecticut."

Cahree shared how she always came back and forth from Colombia to the U.S. with her father when she was a child. "Dis is da first time I have ever been from under my father's thumb. I want to live like an American girl." said the beautiful girl with silky black hair. Petite, but her ass was sitting on 22's and she had breasts to match. She accessorized her outfit well, and her style was similar to Phoenix's.

They became acquainted by sharing their likes and dislikes.

"Whatever joo do, joo never answer my phone. Joo never want to end up having a conversation with me papi. He will have joo obligated to babysit me and joo no want dat." Both agreed the same rule applied to Phoenix's phone. "Me no like many peoples around my things. Bitches are thieves and will steal what dey need and want. What about joo?"

Phoenix laughed. It was like meeting her Colombian twin. "I see we are so much alike, but from different parts of the world. I'm an only child, and I like nice things and want to keep them out of reach from hoodrats."

Cahree looked confused. "Hoodrats? We have rats in here?"

Phoenix laughed again. She knew this semester was going to be cool. "You know, hoodrats? Birds? Chickenheads?"

Cahree still didn't get it. "What joo saying, all dese roam around freely in America?"

Phoenix explained that all of the words she'd used were slang for sneaky bitches who had no upbringing.

"I see I have a lot to learn, but da things joo will learn from me must stay between us."

Cahree began explaining exactly who she was. Her father was a notorious drug lord who supplied most of New York, Miami, and some southern states with cocaine. She had an unlimited budget and was wired money frequently. The only friend she would need was Phoenix. She also told Phoenix if it seemed like men were following them at times, it wasn't because they were the finest chicks on campus. Cahree went on to say that her father had bodyguards and people spying on her. That was fine and dandy with Phoenix. She told Cahree she would just look at them like they were paparazzi. The girls giggled.

"Can I call you 'P'?" Phoenix agreed. Cahree then slid open her phone and said, "Okay."

An entourage of muscular men in wife beaters and fitted denims came in with a truckload of clothing on hangers. They set up her sleigh bed and assembled all of her dressers, leaving their dorm room tight but comfortable.

"Okay, joo ready?" Phoenix had no clue what Cahree was talking about. "Dey are having a party, mami, and we will be dere."

Phoenix hadn't planned on partying, but decided she wasn't going to sit around dwelling on the past. After the girls freshened up, they held each other's hands as they walked to the mixer.

Eyes on the Pryze

Men of all flavors stood in front of the cafeteria. Phoenix and Cahree were turning all the guys' heads and receiving sneers and glares from the women. They loved the attention from everyone. Every now and then, some geek mustered up the courage to ask for their names, if they were seeing anyone. Some even went as far as asking them out on dates. They shot down every one of them.

"Do joo have a boyfriend, P? Cause I see joo don't seem interested in accepting anyone's offer." When Cahree sensed Phoenix's entire mood change, she knew she'd hit on a touchy subject. "I sorry. I no mean to make joo sad. Joo sad or mad?"

Phoenix took a deep breath and shared details of her relationship, or what was once a relationship, with her new friend. "It's okay, Cahree, you didn't know. The answer is no. Not anymore." Phoenix and Cahree took seats on an empty bench while Phoenix continued spilling her guts.

"Wow, so much drama, as joo Americans say! Why he do dat, P? Da way joo talk of him, he no seem like he would do dat. And jor sister, she no seem like it, either. Why joo no find out? Jor father, he a strict man and he let joo have boyfriend? Mi papi no even let me go to school with boys until now."

Phoenix was curious about her love life. "Do you have a boyfriend now? I know you at least took a chance and defied your father. Maybe sneaked and dated?"

Cahree looked at Phoenix as if she'd gone mad. "Are joo crazy! Mi papi would have him killed. Plus, I no want no boyfriend."

When Cahree said that, Phoenix thought she might have been a lesbian. Who could go all their high school years without some kind of boyfriend. A kiss ... a smooch ... something.

"No, P, I'm no girl gone wild. I love men. See, I said no boyfriend. I no need a boy, I need a man. I no come to New York to see boys. I wanna see men. Someone strong and no scared of mi papi. Someone like...Denzel Washington. Joo no think I find him? No?"

Phoenix was relieved. Not that she had something against lesbians, but she wanted a drama-free friend. "Girl, like you said, this is New York. Anything can happen. I've only visited here with my old boyfriend, and a few times to sightsee with my family. But, girl, I know you can find your Denzel."

Cahree told Phoenix how she loved Black men because Colombian men were too bossy and possessive. She then asked Phoenix if she'd like to hit the city and go shopping. "Then we can have lunch on Seventh Avenue in da Village. I love da Village shops."

Phoenix never asked what kind of car Cahree drove, but knew it had to be an expensive one.

"I no drive yet, but we can rent scooters when we go to the Village. We call cab from Park Avenue. Too many bags."

Phoenix felt glad having something that Cahree didn't have. "I drive. Maybe I can teach you on the weekend."

"Joo will? Oh, P, dis is gonna be great!" Cahree gave Phoenix a mini bear hug.

For a while longer, the girls enjoyed the music and snacks their university put out to welcome the students. They tried to mingle, but the campus girls weren't too inviting. They were about to leave when Phoenix heard someone call her name.

Eyes on the Pryze

Who could know me here? She combed the crowd for a familiar face. Lo and behold, a man who looked like Chase from the back, stood by the fountain dead center of the mixer. Phoenix tapped Cahree. "It's him. How'd he find me?"

Cahree looked in the direction Phoenix pointed. "It's who?"

The man had disappeared.

"He was...he was...standing right over there." Phoenix could point out Chase in a New York crowd in a New York minute. But this time she thought she must've been wrong. Maybe she just missed him so much, she was hallucinating. "Never mind."

Cahree wanted to show Phoenix what she planned on wearing the next day.

"Clothes? Now you're talking."

They finished up their drinks and snacks then headed back to their dorm room.

The two tried on each other's clothing and realized that even though they were proportioned differently, they wore the same clothing and shoe size. "Now this is crazy," Phoenix said, "we love the same things and wear the same size. ...Cahree, what do you want in the future?"

Phoenix's question caught Cahree off-guard. Never before had anyone asked what she wanted out of life, or what she wanted—period. It was always what her father expected of her, what he wanted her to do, be, whom to do it with, do it for; but what she wanted—never. Cahree felt vulnerable, unsure if she should share her dreams with Phoenix. She stared at the floor.

"P, dere are things in life we all want for ourselves, and den dere are things in life dat are expected of us. In da life I lead, what I want doesn't matter. With mi papi, I have little choice. Joo do or joo die, and in my family dat means joo are excommunicated from da family. Joo are left out in da world for dead. Death from my family is something I no want."

Phoenix felt sorry for her friend. She couldn't imagine living a life someone else had set up. "Cahree, you said you want to live like an American girl. Well, being American gives you the right to do you. Be you. Live for you. So let's just say that from here on I have adopted you as an American citizen." Phoenix pulled out two wine glasses and poured apple juice in them. They toasted, and Phoenix made Cahree an American citizen. "It's official. Now you can be whatever you want!"

A single tear rolled down Cahree's cheek. "I wish it was dat easy."

"It is that easy! This is America, and we're in New York City. Now, what do you want to be? What's your major?"

"Law. My major is criminal justice, den on to law school."

Cahree didn't strike Phoenix as a stuffed-shirt lawyer type. Phoenix pictured her doing something more creative. "Is that what you want, or what your father wants? Remember, you're an American citizen now. What does the new Carmen want?"

Cahree realized that Phoenix was genuinely interested in what her dreams were. She grew excited then edged over to Phoenix, whispering as if there were other ears in the room. "Fashion. I want to design clothes. Maybe start my own business. A boutique on Rodeo Drive. Something upscale like Gucci, DKNY, Prada. P, dat is my dream. I want my designs worn all over da world. Paris, Italy, da runway, no?"

Phoenix stared at Cahree. Happy to see her friend's eyes glow while she spoke of her dreams, and finally feeling like she was getting to know the real Carmen. "I can't believe this. I want my own boutiques, too! I'm majoring in business first, then design school later. I want to learn the ins and outs of running a business, and I don't want anyone in charge but me."

Phoenix and Cahree gave each other high fives. They talked until both fell asleep in Cahree's bed. Cahree's phone rang at one in the morning. She'd expected this call to come earlier. When it didn't, she assumed she was in for the night.

"Hola?" The voice on the other end told Cahree where to go. "Okay, okay. I said I'll be dere!" Cahree hung up and looked over at Phoenix.

Phoenix tossed then woke. "What's up? Where you going?"

"I have to go," Cahree huffed.

"Go where? You're coming back, right?"

Cahree knew she was coming back, but wanted Phoenix to go with her. She hesitated.

"Well, mi papi sounded upset. I no tell him I live on campus. I don't know how I'm going to explain why it's important to experience campus life. I no think I can stand up for myself and tell him what I want...dat's da hard part."

Phoenix jumped up. "We'll double-team him. It'll sound better coming from both of us. He'll see how important this is to you. Plus, I don't know any dad who can resist a nice girl like me." Phoenix showed Cahree her sweet, innocent schoolgirl look.

Cahree had to laugh. "Mami, joo crazy. It just might work. Get off jor ass. Let's go defeat da big bad wolf. We'll huff and puff—"

"Ain't gon' be no huffing and puffing in here with that breath."

Both girls threw on sweats and their college t-shirts. It was well past their curfew, but Phoenix felt this was worth getting in trouble for. They came up with a game plan to slip out the building unnoticed. Hoping not to be seen, they slid passed security in the lobby. Once outside, they jumped up and down at their victory. They then made their way to the coffee shop to meet with Cahree's father.

The coffee shop was packed, hustling and bustling with people like it was mid-afternoon.

"Don't you just love New York. If we were in Connecticut, it would be like a ghost town this time of morning." New York nightlife fascinated Phoenix. "Let's order something then wait for your dad outside. I saw a table out there."

They approached the counter. The cashier flirted with them a bit before asking for their order. He didn't care who responded; he found them equally beautiful.

"What can I get you, beautiful?"

The girls looked at each other and grinned. "A double shot espres—" they answered at the same time.

"Let me find out you were going to say double shot espresso," Phoenix said.

Cahree's jaw dropped. "Dios mio! Joo are really starting to scare me."

The cashier thought it was too cute. "Don't tell me you two are some sort of twins separated at birth. You've been friends way too long."

"Would you believe we just met today? We're college roommates."

He studied their body language. "No way! You guys even give off the same aura. Either you two are cousins or you've been friends a while."

Phoenix scooped Cahree under her arm and pulled her close. "Nope. We're really lovers," she kissed Cahree's cheek.

"Now that's what I'm talking about!"

They giggled, ordered their espressos, and walked out laughing all the way to their outdoor table.

"Joo are a mess, P. I guess dat stopped him from asking one of us out."

Phoenix caught her breath. "I doubt it. Looking at the bulge in his pants, he might have asked us both out—and probably could've handled us."

"Ooh, girl, joo so nasty."

Phoenix noticed that the mere mention or suggestion of anything sexual embarrassed Cahree. "I know you're not blushing."

Cahree looked away.

"Girl, tell me you're not a virgin. I know you've at least done it once."

"P, don't tease me...no, I never."

Phoenix couldn't believe her ears. "Never?"

"Never! Why did joo? Joo know," Cahree peeked around as though spies were everywhere, "have sex?"

Phoenix had become comfortable with Cahree and decided to share intimate details of her and Chase's past sex life. But Phoenix needed to cross her legs first. Just thinking about sex with him made her clit stiffen.

"Girl, Chase was a sensual lover. It was always about me when we made love. I know all girls think when they're in bed with their man they're making love, but that's not true. Cahree, making love has to do with being in love and it's a two-person thing. Both people have to be in love with each other to bring out the passion required to make love. When you have sex for the first time, if the man isn't willing to make your experience with him a dream come true, he doesn't give a good goddamn!"

Cahree didn't utter a word. This was Sex 101, and she made mental notes.

"Chase was just a runner when I first met him. He sold drugs, but he wasn't a baller. When it was time for us to make love, he went out baller style. We got a hotel suite with a Jacuzzi in it. Chase set the room up with trails of my favorite candy, Hershey's Kisses, and rose petals that led to my pillow. He had non-alcoholic sparkling cider chilling because he doesn't drink or get high. He took me to bed and undressed me and then carried me to the bathroom. And, girl, the tub had milk in it and floating candles. He even had petals floating in the water. He bathed and then dried me off. Then he gave me a massage with shea butter. I loved it."

Cahree sat enthralled with Phoenix's reminiscence. She could tell Phoenix wasn't making the whole thing up because she noticed equal tears and passion in Phoenix's eyes.

Eyes on the Pryze

"He fed me strawberries dipped in chocolate that was dripping from this fountain thing. He kissed my entire body.

"Girl, it was my first time, so I didn't know much. My fast-ass girlfriends always told me stories about oral sex, but I never knew it would be so good when he, uh, licked my stuff. I felt like crying. It felt so good. My boyfr, I mean, Chase didn't leave one spot on my body not licked or sucked." Phoenix giggled, "even my toes. I gave him a massage. It felt so natural, I even touched his, well, you know. I massaged that, too, then we made love all night long. It was my prom night."

Cahree could picture it all in her mind, just like all the romance novels she's read.

"Did joo give him oral sex?"

Her question embarrassed Phoenix. That wasn't something you could tell just anyone; some people have negative outlooks on things like that. "Well, not that night." Phoenix left it at that.

"Wow. Den why joo no love him no more? Why joo think he a bad man? He sounds like a good man. Maybe joo should—"

Phoenix couldn't hold back her tears. She tried, but she still loved him. "I'm just not—"

He appeared again. He walked right by her.

"What? What's wrong, P?"

By the time Phoenix was able to speak, he disappeared.

"He must've turned down that block. Come on!" She grabbed Cahree's hand. "Come on, girl. It's Chase!" Cahree picked up her pocketbook and ran with her.

"I thought joo said he doesn't know where joo are."

Phoenix spotted him standing on the edge of the sidewalk. "See? It is him, waving."

A cab pulled to the curb, and he was gone just as fast as he'd appeared.

Phoenix dropped her arms in frustration. "I know that was him."

"How? He was so far away."

Phoenix didn't bother explaining to her naïve friend how she could pick Chase out of a crowd of a thousand lookalikes. She knew she wouldn't understand. "I just know." Missing Chase by a split second was killing her. She wanted to call him, but refused to make the first step. She wanted Chase to be the first to explain and apologize. "Oh, my god...your father."

"He's probably not coming. He's like that. Let's go."

Phoenix checked her watch. Time went by so fast. It was already five in the morning. She knew once they reached the dorm, there would be no time for her to get a bit more rest. She wanted to be out bright and early to get first dibs on picking classes. When they arrived back at their dorm, the Resident Assistant awaited them at the front desk.

"We have a mandatory curfew here, ladies. Violations of the policy will get you kicked out on your rich little butts. I'll let this go as a warning, but the next will be a violation. Three violations will result in suspension. After that it's goodbye." The RA looked at Cahree, "Adios. Read your policy and procedure manuals I gave you both yesterday."

They headed to their dorm room silently mimicking the RA's body language.

"Whatever. Why does she think we're rich?"

"Cause we are. Joo rich in experience, me rich in dollars."

"Let's get washed up and dressed, so we can get a bite then go register for class. Have you picked out what you're going to take?"

Cahree proudly handed Phoenix a list of classes she jotted down. Phoenix's eyes widened.

"I do right by my citizenship."

Phoenix hugged her friend. Except for two, Cahree's classes were identical to Phoenix's. "Damn right, my American friend! Do you! Now let's get ready so we can try to get the same class schedule....What are you going to tell your father?"

"I'm not."

After choosing their classes, they spent the rest of the afternoon shopping on 125th Street, and had their hair done. New York was an adventure for Phoenix. Phoenix was an adventure for Cahree. From that point on, they became inseparable.

"Let's ride the subway," Phoenix suggested. "I never got the chance to do that."

"Me, either."

They didn't enjoy being crammed against strangers, and the thickness of the air was less than desirable. When they returned to their dorm room, Phoenix noticed the red light blinking on her answering machine. The caller ID displayed a few calls as private. No messages were left by the private numbers. The last call and only message came from home. Phoenix picked up her phone to call her mother and introduce her to her new sistah-friend.

"Hey, mom. Just calling to let you know all is well. How's everything? How's daddy?"

Her mom confessed that her father was worried sick about her, especially when he received a phone call from a lady in the financial aid department at her old college inquiring about where to transfer her aid.

"He thought they may have cut off your aid since they didn't know where you were, and that you wouldn't have a place to stay. You know he'll always think of you as his baby girl. So how's college life in New York? Meet any new people?"

"Mom, my aid was transferred months ago. No one would have called you from financial aid. What did you and Daddy tell them? Did they leave a number?" Phoenix's mom relayed details of the conversation to her daughter. Phoenix then said, "Okay, mom, I'll call you back," and hung up then explained the strange incident to Cahree.

"Seems like jor knight in armor does care," Cahree said. She then walked into the bathroom, where she made a private call.

Phoenix, now completely convinced that the guy who disappeared on her twice was definitely Chase, didn't know what she'd say when he finally approached her. All she could do was sleep on it.

"Rise and shine, mami! We have our day planned. Remember, bookstore, school supplies? I need a laptop."

Phoenix rolled over throwing the comforter over her head.

"Uh, uh, uh, we have to go. P, we're gonna get da leftover books." Cahree pulled the comforter off Phoenix. "Get up!"

Eyes on the Pryze

Phoenix had no choice. She looked over at Cahree humming and smiling like Mary Poppins. How does she do that? She could get an hour's sleep and be bright and perky in the morning. I want what she's taking. Phoenix didn't feel like getting too fashionable, considering she was still tired and they were only going to get books and other supplies. She threw on her college sweat shorts and a tank top. She then pulled her hair into a ponytail topped off with a baseball cap. "Ta da! Ready?"

Cahree shook her head at Phoenix's attire. "Whatever floats jor boat, but me, I am looking for my Denzel."

The lines were long.

"We should've eaten breakfast."

Cahree, shifting in her stilettos, looked at Phoenix as if she was crazy. "And what do joo think the lines would've been like, den? My feet are killing me."

"I warned you not to wear those heels. Sit down. I'll hold our place."

After a few minutes of sitting, Cahree limped out the crowded, stuffy bookstore to get some air. Seconds later, she ran back in the store in a frenzy. Phoenix tried to make out what Cahree was trying to tell her, then she heard Chase's name. She ran out of the store with her friend in tow.

He was coming toward her. Something was different about his walk...stiffer. Something was different about his face...just different. Phoenix sat on one of the benches in front of the bookstore and tried to look normal. She stared him in his face. He walked right by her; didn't speak or even look at her more than a second.

61

Felisha Bradshaw

What? This niggah lost his mind? I know he doesn't expect me to say something first. Phoenix sat on her hands and rocked back and forth, trying to stop herself from jumping up—getting all in his face. Stay calm. Just stay calm.

Cahree looked on. "Dere he is—right dere!" Why isn't she getting up? "Go!" Cahree signaled to Phoenix, pushing the air as if she could shove her friend in that direction. Phoenix didn't budge. She sat, rocking back and forth like someone with a nervous condition. Now, dis girl is stubborn! Phoenix continued rocking with her hands beneath her until he was out of her sight. Cahree was afraid to touch her. The anger and hurt in her eyes could blow up half of New York City.

Phoenix's animosity toward Chase grew to its highest height that day. She vowed when Chase stopped playing mind games and approached her, she was going to give him a serious beat down.

Cahree wisely gave Phoenix time to herself and waited for her to come out of bitch mode. She knew that love mixed with hurt and anger could turn a person for the worse. "I'll go get our books. When joo ready, I will be here for joo."

It took Cahree an hour to gather the books and supplies they needed for class. She retrieved a cart to lug all the materials. When she returned to the bench, Phoenix was gone. Cahree looked about the crowd in search of her friend's baseball cap. Phoenix was nowhere to be found. "Ugh!" Cahree ate lunch then took a cab back to their dorm room. She found it empty.

Phoenix wandered around the Village with no particular destination in mind. She must think I'm a fool. All

Eyes on the Pryze

the stories I told her about the great Chase Pryze and his love for me...she must think I'm a fool.

Phoenix took a seat on a bench in Washington Square Park and watched the old heads play chess. She watched so long, she could have won a game herself; although she'd never played chess before. A stout Mexican lady walked by pushing a melon cart, so Phoenix purchased lunch. She calmed down by the time the food settled on her stomach. *Guess I'll go face the music.* Phoenix stood to leave. She took one step without looking and bumped directly into him. Both fell, with Phoenix landing on top of him. "You sorry son-of-a-bitch! What! Are you stalking me! You trying to drive me crazy!" With each word she spoke, she landed a punch to his body.

He grabbed control of her hands, flipped her over, and pinned her down on her back.

"Ay, gal! Mi no know whatta gwan wit choo. Why ya lick mi so?" he struggled to contain her. "Yuh muss behave ya self, seen? Stop gwan like mad 'oman!"

Phoenix stared at the man she'd attacked. He bore no scar on his cheek, just the few minor scratches she'd given him. His eyes were not Chase's. His voice, not Chase's, but everything else belonged to Chase.

"I, I, I'm sorry. Please get off of me."

"Mi gwan let yuh free, seen? But if yuh start de fuckery..." he rose off her then held out his hand to help her up.

"I can explain." Phoenix introduced herself. They took a seat on the bench while she told this complete stranger her story.

"So, yuh nuh crazy?"

Phoenix assured him, "No, just a woman scorned. I wish I'd kept a picture of him so you could see what I'm talking about." Phoenix moved closer. She reached out to touch his face. He grabbed her wrist. "Please?" He allowed Phoenix to touch the side of his face that should have had a scar. "You could be his identical twin. I swear. You more than look like someone who just favors him from far away. You're a spitting image of him up close. This is amazing. I can't believe it."

"Well, Miss Phoenix, mi muss say mi nevah been attacked by a 'oman so beautiful." He wiped his hand on his jeans then held it out to shakes hers. She held his hand in hers so long he placed his other hand on top. "Dem call mi Caine. Even though yuh lick mi wit fire, mi still glad to meet yuh."

"Did you say Caine?"

He nodded, "Excuse mi accent."

Phoenix shook her head, "No, no. Chase is Jamaican, too. I understand every word you're saying. It's just...your names seem like names you'd give to twins, you know? He's Chase, you're Caine. Chase and Caine. This is just amazing."

His smile could have lit up three New York City blocks during a blackout. "Mi know. Yuh said it before." Caine tried to curb his accent; he wanted to take her mind off her old boyfriend. "Where were yuh going? Cyan I walk yuh dere?"

She allowed him to return her to the bookstore.

Phoenix and Caine took to each other instantly. The only time she wasn't by his side was when she had class or spent time with Cahree. She habitually broke curfew to be with him. When the infractions added up, Phoenix was called to the RA's office and asked to leave. Phoenix didn't have to beg Cahree to go with her. When she returned to their dorm room, all of their things were packed. Phoenix was surprised to find Cahree's father's goons there—awaiting her return. Phoenix looked at Cahree.

"Hey, I just knew!"

CHASE

Chase sat in his two-bedroom apartment staring at pictures of Phoenix. Not knowing her whereabouts was driving him mad. He thought she'd give into him by now. Chase picked up his phone and tried calling her again, knowing what the outcome would be.

"Hi, Mom, is Phoenix home?" Chase waited for her rehearsed answer.

"Chase, baby, I wish I could tell you what's going on with Phoenix, but I can't. I still love you like a son; everybody makes mistakes. I tried to talk to Phoenix about what was troubling her, but you know how she is. Just like her daddy, stubborn as a mule. But I will tell you this: Phoenix no longer lives at home. Listen to your heart, boy, and you'll figure it all out. I wish I could tell you more but, baby, I just can't. She'd never forgive me."

Chase heard the sincerity in her voice. He began to cry. He truly loved Phoenix and always believed that she'd been placed on this earth just for him.

"Mom, I'd never hurt Phoenix. Never. I'd leave her before I let anything or anyone hurt her. Even if it's me or someone going through her to get to me. You know that, right?"

"Baby, I know. I know. But I'm not the one who needs to hear this, she is."

Eyes on the Pryze

Chase sobbed into the phone. "But I don't even know what I did wrong. We were fine one minute, she was refusing my calls the next. What did I do, Ma, what did I do?"

"Baby, like I said, if you think, you'll know where to look. You know her just as well as us...including Vina." She couldn't bear hearing him cry, but couldn't give him any further information. She prayed he'd heed her words. "Goodbye Chase."

Chase couldn't hang up the phone. He sat for an hour with it in his hand. Gone? Where did she go? Why would she just up and leave? Chase didn't pick up on the hints Phoenix's mother tried giving him. He questioned himself to sleep, forgetting to hang up the phone.

Nigel tried to reach Chase again. "Boss, please, mi need yuh fi pick up de line...cha! Call mi, seen?"

Cutty also left a message on Chase's voice mail. "Bredren, mi gwan call de yard. Answer de phone." Cutty called the house phone. Still no answer. He decided that once he touched base with his squad and made his pickup and drop-off rounds, he'd check in on his young, dear friend.

The aggravating tone of the phone off the hook woke Chase. From his sofa, he looked out the living room window and noticed the sun beginning to set. Come on, man, think. Who would know more than me? Vina came to mind. He started to call, but decided this should be done in person. He jumped up and left his apartment, unintentionally leaving behind his pager and cell phone. When he reached the parking garage, he realized that he also left his keys in his apartment with the automatic lock. "Fuck it! I'll cab it." He reached for his phone to call a cab, and now realized he forgot that, too. "Damn! God, you know I never thought once to ever ask you for anything but, right now, I need for you to do what you do best."

His neighbor pulled up. A simple what's up from his neighbor gave Chase an avenue to spill out all his grief. Chase couldn't believe he told a guy he never said more than two words to his dilemma.

"Yo, cuz, anything for love," his neighbor handed over the keys to his Jeep Grand Cherokee.

Chase thanked his neighbor. He held the keys tightly in his palm, looked up and nodded, "Thanks."

Vina was sitting on her front porch while some guy played with Phillie's dog on the front lawn. Damn burbs!

Chase hopped out the truck, trying to keep his emotions intact. Butch heard the gate's hinge squeak. She immediately stopped playing. She stood guard over Vina and Phillie.

"Yo, V, I know you told me you were handling feeling safe, but damn! That bitch is a beast."

Once she saw it was Chase, Phillie grabbed Butch's collar and walked her to the backyard. Vina didn't say much to him. She was in no mood for company.

"What's good, V? Was that Phillisha Brasshaw from around the block?" Chase avoided looking up at Phoenix's bedroom window.

"Yeah. You know she hates that name, so stick to Phillie." Vina stared at Phoenix's window.

"I ain't seen you in a minute, and that's how you show your brother love?" Chase followed her eyes. "Has she called you to explain why she hates me?"

Eyes on the Pryze

"Talk to me? Talk to me? Phoenix hasn't talked to me since the night before Blizz and his boys raped me. Maybe she—"

Chase's eyes had fire in them. "Blizz? You talking about that punk that runs the No Dough Boys! What makes you think he was one?"

Vina finally came clean with Chase and told him she'd been dealing with Blizz for a minute and he'd come over that night to get smoked. Phillie took a seat next to Vina, nodding at Chase. Then she nodded at Vina, letting her know it was okay to tell Chase everything. Vina continued.

"Blizz told Phillie that I invited her and the Dough Boys over for a smoke session."

Chase knew those niggahs were grimy, but not like that. The more Vina went into detail, the angrier he became. "And his punk ass videoed it? Vina, you know what time it is, right?" The way he looked at Vina let her know that he was unsure if he could discuss business in front of Phillie. Vina's nod eased his concerns. "Yo, V, he has to get it."

Vina told Chase she wanted to get the tape back from Blizz before they took his ass out. Chase wanted to be included and promised to put someone on it right away.

"Has Rajii checked in with you yet?"

Just hearing his name made Chase's trigger finger twitch. "Nah. That little niggah is dead to me...ta roti. 'im dead, seen, star?" Chase glanced up at Phoenix's window every so often, hoping to hear her yell out his name any minute.

Vina smirked hearing Chase's Jamaican accent come out. That was rare around them. "I see you keep staring at that window. Why isn't she talking to you?"

69

Chase's shoulders slumped. "I thought you'd be able to fill me in. I know I didn't return her calls when she hit me up, but I had that Rajii shit to take care of. When I left here that night, I was scared to go around her because I gave you my word. I knew if I went around her she'd know something was up. Right after I left you, she called me and asked where I was. I lied and told her I was on the other side of town, and she freaked out! She hung up on me and I haven't spoken to her ever since. Not that I haven't tried, she just won't accept my calls."

Vina knew this was too much of a coincidence. "You know, she stopped talking to me that same night. I didn't try to call her until the next day, but she wouldn't talk to me. I went over and she refused to say anything to me. She didn't even open her room door."

After retracing each step they made, they both wondered if Phoenix saw him carry her into the house.

"Nah, she'd never think that. I'm her sis."

Chase's face tightened. "You? I'm her man...or I was."

Both realized that Phoenix had to have seen them.

"She had to be in her window. You know, that girl always could hear your Benz from a mile away like she had super powers," Vina smiled at the thought of her friend.

"I know. I could never surprise her with a visit. V, we have to find her and explain this shit. I knew giving my word would come back to bite me in the ass."

"Have you tried talking to her moms?"

"You know, come to think of it, she was trying to give me hints without betraying Phoenix's trust. I can't believe I let that slip right by me until now. Something told me to come to you when she asked who would know Phoenix as much as I do. But the rest went in one ear and out the other."

"Yo," Phillie blurted, "her car was packed to max. She even had a mini U-Haul truck. I saw her dad packing all sorts of shit in it. Vina was way too out of it to notice. She was crying and all cause Phoenix was igging her."

"What did he put in the truck?"

"I remember a computer desk and a big box with a picture of a futon on it. There were a bunch of different size boxes. Yo, I bet she was going to school. It was right before the semester started." Phillie saw a ray a hope gleam across Vina's face. She and Vina had grown close. Seeing her happy was worth a million dollars to Phillie. She tried to help even more. "First, you guys need to go to Housatonic and see if she still there, and she didn't just get her own crib."

Chase shook his head. "We don't need to worry about that. Her father would never let her do that. I got a plan. Phillie, you got a cell phone?"

Phillie reached on her hip and handed her phone to Chase.

"Nah. You dial Phoenix's mom's line and tell her you're calling from the financial aid office at Housatonic and there's been some trouble sending her aid to her new college. Maybe she'll give us the name of her school. Sound professional, mom dukes ain't no idiot."

Vina jumped up and hugged Chase. "My big brother ain't no joke when that crazy ass brain of his starts ticking."

Phillie followed Chase's instructions, and it worked. Phoenix's mom even gave her the phone number to her daughter's dorm room.

"Wait a few then call her moms back to let her know things went smoothly, so she doesn't worry."

"NYU here we come! I'm gonna get my sister back!" Vina turned and laid a big tongue kiss on Phillie.

Chase couldn't believe his eyes. "Let me find out..."

"Find out what? Vina asked slyly. "That's right, I'm repping the rainbow!" Vina kissed Phillie again. This time to make their relationship official. "She has treated me better than any niggah ever has. We gonna do this, right, Phillie?"

Phillie was still in shock from the initial kiss. All she could do was nod in agreement.

The news didn't bother Chase. "Long as you're happy, I'm happy. So, when are we leaving? I have a few things to take care of, but as far as anything more important that seeing my girl, there's nothing!"

Chase used Phillie's cell to hit up Cutty. "Yo, mon, mi tired of callin dis phone and yuh no dere, seen? Mi done wit de fuckery! Mi wan de Rajii business done! Yuh 'ear mi, star? Mi muss mek a run to de city. Mi soon check yuh. Keep tings irie. Likkle more."

"We'll be ready in a sec," Vina said.

Chase sat on the porch and waited for Vina and Phillie. Things were looking up.

Phillie and Vina walked into the house to begin packing. Phillie shared three words with Vina. "I love you."

TO CATCH A THIEF: First Attempt

Three-five-seven Heavy Hitters went their separate ways the night Cutty put the pounds on Rajii's head. Even though they were once homies, this meant nothing when someone is shunned from the crew. Rajii had committed two of the highest violations under their ride or die oath: betrayal and theft.

Mad Mike called his peoples in the Terrace. They claimed there was no new head on the grind named Rajii with the Dough Boys. Striking a dead end, he knew he'd have to take that ride himself. Mike rented a low-key midsize car and rode throughout the Terrace.

This lil niggah seems like he jumped off the face of the earth. I didn't know he had it in him. Just when Mike was about to leave, the bass from an Escalade caught his attention. The truck slowly pulled up to a dealer with the Dough Boys crew.

Nah, that ain't Raj. No fitted, no jersey, and this niggah got niggahs slinging for him. Mike couldn't get a good look at his face, but instinct told him to standby. Since the Terrace was one strip with parking lots running off of it, Mike knew the Escalade had to pass him on its way out. Mike reclined his seat and waited. Nah! Stop playing! Rajii's living it up and done got brand new with 357's money. Oh, hell no!

Felisha Bradshaw

Rajii parked his truck in the lot and climbed out. "This shit is bananas," Mike referred to Rajii's slick new look. "He's gotta get it!" It wasn't so much that Rajii robbed 357, Mike was hating on how well Rajii pulled it off and was now living it up. For a split second, he wished he was Rajii —until he remembered the hit. "Thanks for the twenty G's."

Mike took aim at Rajii and let shots ring, paying no mind to the little boy riding by on his scooter. The crowd dispersed like roaches; Mike was spraying Raid.

Rajii dived behind an abandoned car and pulled Nina from his waist. Shots rang until no bullets were left. The Dough Boys ran for cover then joined in to help their comrade, hitting Mike numerous times in his upper body and riddling his rental with bullets.

Mike tried to drive off. Kye came out of nowhere spraying an oozy, leaving Mike slumped over the steering wheel. Kye walked slowly to the driver's side of the car, never taking his finger off the trigger. He opened the car door and Mike fell to the earth. Kye then vamped his chain and the rest of Mike's jewelry. Then he emptied his pockets of a small knot of money, and sprayed him with more bullets. By the time the police arrived, Mike was unrecognizable.

"Yo, Shop, you a'ight?"

Rajii was frozen stiff. He was a thug on the surface, but today he was made to question his status. Yeah, he carried Nina at all times, but he never had to use her. Just having her made him feel safe. He knew now that Nina was going to have to step up her game. His life depended on it. "Yeah, man, I'm a'ight. But—" Rajii pointed to the little boy lying two feet away from him. He gasped for air while holding his throat where the bullet had entered. His small hands covered with blood. What his hands could not stop from running, squirted into the air. Rajii slid over to him. "Hold on, lil man. We're gonna get you help, a'ight? Be a soldier for me. Just don't try to talk." The young boy gave a slight nod. Rajii looked up at the crowd forming around the boy. "Where the fuck is his mother! Who knows where he lives!"

Sirens coming from ambulance trucks and police cars drowned out the crowd's whispers. Rajii eased into the crowd. Because he was too busy with the little boy, he never got a glimpse at the man who caused all this to happen. The coroner arrived on scene and pulled a white sheet over the boy's tiny body. Rajii knew his little soldier had fallen.

The Dough Boys spat on the ground. "Niggahs should know we ain't having it!"

"Yo, Shop," Kye pulled Rajii aside, "was that for you?"

Rajii knew the answer to that question, but wasn't ready to admit it. Chase sent that niggah out here. I know it. I was his man...now he wants me dead. "Nah, man. I wasn't able to get a look at him. I don't think I know that niggah."

Kye took his word for it. It wasn't like this was the first time rivals tried to test the Dough Boys...nor would it be the last. "You think that kid made it? I never seen no shit like that."

Rajii shot Kye a look. He found that hard to believe, considering the way he ran up on that car like he was Scarface. "Nah, I knew he wasn't going to make it. I think he knew, too...I could see it in his eyes." Rajii changed the subject. "Yo, I gotta keep my eye on your ass. Y'all quiet muthafuckahs are scandalous."

Felisha Bradshaw

Kye knew Rajii didn't expect him to be so ruthless. As far as Kye was concerned, you live or die in the streets. He was only trying to live. "Me?" Kye tried to appear meek. "I was a monster, huh?" he gave Rajii a playful shove.

"Yeah a'ight, Scarface," Rajii mimicked Kye holding the oozy.

"Say hello to my little friend!" Kye pulled out the jewelry and money he took off Mike's body. "Here, man, you like this shit. I'll keep the dough."

Rajii respected Kye from that moment on. Rajii knew that Kye didn't have to show him what he lifted off the body, but he did. That let Rajii know that Kye was a man he could trust. Rajii took the jewelry and chucked it in his back pocket, but not before noticing the ruby studded scorpion medallion swinging on the chain. He knew then that his would-be hitman was Mad Mike. He felt bad that it was Mike because he'd taught him part of the game.

It didn't take but a few seconds after the kid was hauled off to a basement freezer at the local morgue for these two thugs to forget about the pitfalls of their lifestyle. A lifestyle where death stood in the shadows lurking for its next victim, with no regard for age.

SECOND ATTEMPT

News rushed back to the 357 crew that the Dough Boys killed one of their men. None of the chosen Heavy Hitters were aware that Mike rode into enemy territory, alone, to take out Rajii. They wanted revenge.

Cutty decided to try contacting Chase again. Chase answered in the midst of throwing a few things in a bag for his trip to the city. Cutty finally caught up with him.

"Get ready fi sen Mike's muddah flowers. 'im gone. Dey killed 'im."

Chase slumped down on the couch. "Yo, why you send him out? Mi plan fi give 'im Nigel's position. Now yuh tek care of 'is business. Did yuh get de message?"

"Yeah, mon. Check de cell fuh mi. Mi call yuh twenty time." Chase explained briefly that he located Phoenix. "Yo, mon, whatta gwan? Phoenix missin? Mi nevah know."

Chase assured Cutty that he was handling things and everything would be alright. "But fuh yuh, business as usual. Call mi when tings turn up." Chase hung up.

On the other end of the phone, Cutty grew frustrated. He was dedicated to Chase, but knew he was slipping. Now, losing one of their best men put more weight on Cutty. Cutty wanted this Rajii shit over with, so he made a decision without Chase's approval. He gathered all the Heavy Hitters again and told them he was taking the hit in another direction. Cutty then went on a three-day fast.

He wanted his mind clear and his body hungry. "Rajii, yuh dead, mon!"

Nigel caught wind of what happened to Mike and was pleased. He saw it as a chance to earn back his position in 357. Catching Rajii in the Terrace was out of the question. Rajii had too many niggahs watching his back. Nigel wasn't the best trigger man, nor was he ready to die. In order to catch Rajii, Nigel needed a plan within a plan. He needed to catch Rajii alone and vulnerable.

IN SEARCH OF LOVE

Chase used Phillie's cell phone to call Cutty again while still waiting for Vina and Phillie to pack just a few things. "Yo, mi pray yuh gwan handle tings. Yuh muss do dey pickups. Gwan to de spot and get de candy fi all de shops and keep a record in de books. Latah."

What the fuck is up with him? Chase wasn't going to allow Cutty's bullshit stop the rush he got just thinking about seeing Phoenix again, and setting things straight.

Meanwhile, Phillie loaded up Vina's Land Rover with all the suitcases Vina packed. Just like a woman, Phillie thought. We're just going across the way to New York and she acts like we're going on vacation. Vina was feeling good for the first time in a while. She was going to get her sister back, plus she found that special someone. Things couldn't get any better.

Chase thought more on Vina's being involved with another woman. Who knew!

"Chase, we have to take Butch back to Phillie's house. Who knows how long we'll be in the city."

"Y'all follow me. I have to get some things for myself." Chase then remembered that he'd locked himself out his apartment. He then remembered that he'd given Phoenix a spare key to his crib. Hope it's in the same place. "I gotta go across the street to get my key. Just a sec."

Phoenix's mom came to the door. "Boy, you know she's not here. Did you not hear anything I said to you?" With a wide grin, Chase told her he was just there for his spare key, and told her where to find it. She returned minutes later with his key. "Good luck, son, and I mean it." She hugged him then sent him on his way.

Chase was just as bad as Vina when it came to grabbing just a few things. He threw his bags in back while Vina and Phillie shook their heads.

"What?"

"You're worse than me."

Chase laughed then shared that he would propose to Phoenix once they straightened out this misunderstanding. "Check this out. It's just a little sumpum sumpum." He handed Vina the small velvet box. "I've been holding this ring for about six months. I wanted to give it to her on her birthday, but I, I don't know. I just didn't. Whacha think?"

"Dayum, Chase, this had to cost you a grip! A little sumpum sumpum, yeah right! Now that's what I call bling bling." Vina recognized the ring as Phoenix's dream ring that she kept a picture of in her diary. "Ooh, I'm telling! You been in Phoenix's diary."

"How do you think I know her so well? I had to know if she loved me just as much as I love her. You know how she is. She would have never shown me."

Phillie dipped in and out of New York traffic.

"You're just as wild as these New Yorkers." Phillie's wild driving had Chase sliding from one side of the back seat to the other. "Where we gonna stay until we track down Phoenix?" Chase leaned forward, balancing himself by holding both front seat headrests. "Pick any place. It's on me."

Phillie smiled. "Since you put it that way, Hotel Chelsea here we come."

Vina looked over at Phillie; she never ceased to amaze her. "What you know about New York or the Chelsea?"

Phillie schooled Vina on Greenwich Village. "NYU is in the heart of the Village. I know that area like I know," she glided her hand between Vina's thighs. Vina blushed.

"Yo, could y'all hold out on that shit. I'm just getting used to the whole situation. I know Phoenix is gonna be shocked."

Vina wasn't worried about that. She knew Phoenix was respectful of all lifestyles. They had many gay friends at Laurelton Hall. Spending their first two years of high school at an all girls school opened their minds to the girl-on-girl thing.

After they checked into Hotel Chelsea, Chase was ready to find the love of his life. Vina and Phillie agreed to stay behind so Chase could spend some private time with Phoenix. "I'll call you soon as I find her. Promise." Vina hugged Chase and wished him luck.

Phillie took Vina to the Pier. She couldn't believe how acceptable the gay lifestyle was there. Men were coupled up with men; women coupled with women—out in the open. It seemed like a gay meeting ground. A place to feel comfortable without the criticism. A small city within a city. They took a romantic walk along the Pier, talking about their hopes and dreams.

Vina confessed to Phillie that since her parents died, she hadn't thought about her future. She blocked out many things by hanging out at clubs and smoking.

"Ever since the, well, you know, I've been thinking more and more about my future. I inherited some money, but I never thought about what to do with it. I just thought the money would always be there. Just like I thought my parents would be." Vina stopped and looked out on the water. "Phoenix and I always talked about starting her own clothing line. She wanted to call it "Chasing Phoenix". She had an idea for the logo and all. It was footsteps and a Phoenix. I was going to be the accountant. You know, the business side of the business. I was going to start college with her, but then my folks died. Now that I have the money to do what I want, I don't know what I want. What about you?"

"It was hard coming-out to my parents. I contemplated suicide and everything."

Vina thought about how hard it must have been for her to do that, having church-going parents; especially with her dad being a deacon. Vina's parents were really down-to-earth, yet she didn't know how she would tell them if they were still alive. "How did you tell them?"

Phillie laughed now, but at the time it was the worst time of her young life. "Remember that girl, Chicas, I was always with when we went to Laurelton Hall?"

"Wasn't she your best friend?"

"It started out like that. She'd stay over my house, I'd stay over hers. Then one night, she slept over and we were talking about who were the cutest chicks at school, and who just looked fucked up. She said she thought I was cute. I never knew why I got goosebumps whenever she laid up against me in my bed...until she kissed me. And I mean tongue and all. We started touching each other and one thing led to another and my mom walked in. She liked to have a heart attack. She screamed and ran out my room then in came my father. He grabbed Chicas by the arm and took her home in her pajamas. I tried to call her to see what happened, but she never returned my calls. When I went back to school, her parents had taken her out of Laurelton Hall. I even went by her house. Her mother cussed me out, forbidding me to see her. I cried forever.

"We started sneaking around, but it just got too hectic. So she went her way and I went mine. My parents didn't speak to me for like three months. That's when I tried to kill myself. Then they slowly came around. I remember them saying it was a phase. They blamed it on me being around nothing but girls. That's why I didn't come back for junior year."

"So, is it a phase?"

Phillie smiled. "If it is, it's the longest phase I've ever known anyone to go through. I think it was their way of coping with it. Calling it a phase made it seem temporary."

Phillie then shared her dream of becoming a counselor for gay teens or opening a gay club or restaurant. Never before had Vina felt so happy just being herself. She dropped her guard, praying that she was doing the right thing.

Chase stopped at the registrar's office hoping that Phoenix hadn't blacklisted him there the way she did everywhere else. He was told that student records were confidential. Fortunately, he knew which dorm she lived in thanks to her mom, but the campus was huge. Chase told the front desk lady he was there to see Phoenix Hargrove after signing the visitor's log.

"Phoenix no longer lives at the dorm. Sorry, sir."

Chase knew he was going to need help finding her. He called Vina and Phillie and told them to meet him in Washington Square Park.

PHOENIX

"Wow! This is the bomb."

Phoenix tried not to seem like she had never been anywhere, but this was Yo MTV Crib, Pimp My Place, Mr. Belvedere, and Lifestyles of the Rich and Famous shit all wrapped in one. Damn, how rich is Cahree?

"I hope joo'll be comfortable." Cahree knew she would; she was just being polite.

"Is this your father's place? I was just going to rent a one bedroom or something, I saw a few postings on the student information board about people looking for roommates. You didn't have to call your dad."

Phoenix was glad that she did. She knew she couldn't afford a place in New York nor did she want to have a new roommate.

"Nah. It belongs to a friend of his." Cahree slumped on the couch. "Joo wanna stay in da same room ... we can both sleep in da loft."

Phoenix looked around the brownstone. This was something she had to get used to. "Yeah, that's straight. This place is way big, and I like our talks before bed. Don't you?"

Cahree never had a close friend that wasn't appointed by her father. She grew so close to P in such a short time, it was like having a sister. "Joo don't know da half of it. Let's get our stuff unpacked and den we can raid da fridge. We still going to da club with Caine tonight?" Cahree was trying too hard to do the new Jamaican dance, the Dirty Wind.

"Girl, you gonna break your neck. Yeah. I can't wait; this is our twentieth date. But something just doesn't seem right. He hasn't made a pass at me or even touched anything more than my hand. I thought New York men were more aggressive."

Cahree tried to convince Phoenix that Caine was just probably being a gentleman.

"Aren't joo freaked out dat he looks so much like Chase?"

Phoenix had taken that into consideration. At one point, it was all that she saw. Caine did look like he could be Chase's identical twin, but he was more laid back and had a softer appearance because he didn't have a scar on his cheek. For those reasons, Phoenix saw something different. To her he was just Caine.

"You know, Cahree, I did think it was crazy strange. But now that I'm getting to know Caine, he's so different from Chase, I don't think about it. We've been skating and bike riding in Central Park. He took me to the Statue of Liberty. I'm not saying Chase and I didn't do things together, but it was different.

"Chase and I laid around each other. We'd occasionally do the movie thing. We shopped, stayed in my room watching rented movies. You couldn't dare get Chase on a bike. What he and I did I loved, but this is more... How can I put it? More mature. You know what I mean?"

Cahree didn't exactly know what she meant by experience, but she knew it was what she wanted for herself.

"When me and Denzel hook up, dat's what we'll be on ... some grown folks only adventures."

Phoenix and Cahree tried on outfits, seeing what looked the hottest. Phoenix was out to impress Caine; Cahree was just out to impress. Phoenix settled for a black low cut dress, revealing just a hint of the package she was carrying. The dress showed off a little cleavage and came just above the knee, with her back out. With Cahree's help, her makeup was flawless. Cahree lent her a pair of black stilettos that strapped up her calf, to make it all complete. Basically, Cahree transformed her into the woman she knew she was. The finishing touches were complete. Phoenix swirled around, showing off her new look. She was so used to the 'round-the-way girl look, but tonight she felt like a new woman.

"Joo look so beautiful!" Cahree guided P to the full-length mirror.

"I feel beautiful." Phoenix knew she wasn't ugly, but never did she think she could look so sophisticated. "Girl, you don't look too bad yourself. You're rocking that Vera Wang. Guess you won't be Dirty Winding tonight." Cahree strutted her stuff like she was on the runway. P followed, "We're such fucking ladies."

Cahree thought Phoenix just said the funniest thing. "P, joo are so crazy!"

Phoenix called Caine to tell him they were ready. It wasn't long before he rang their bell.

"Oh, my God. Oh, my God. He's here, he's here!" excited, Phoenix did a pirouette.

"Girl, joo should let me answer da door, so joo can make an entrance. Plus, joo need to get jorself together. Go touch up jor lips and calm down before joo start sweating."

Phoenix agreed, calm down, calm down. P walked back upstairs and sat on the edge of the tub, waiting for Cahree to announce her gentleman caller.

"Phoenix, jor date is here!"

Phoenix came downstairs with one hand on the banister, slowly approaching her date. She silently prayed that she would make it down without tripping. (You know shit like that always happens).

Caine stared up at Phoenix. Damn! Each moment with Phoenix made him hate Chase even more. Caine elegantly took her by the hand and twirled her around, holding one hand behind his back. Phoenix felt like a princess going to the ball, while Caine took in all her assets. "You look marvelous! You're beautiful!" His smile could light up any room. He removed his hand from behind his back, revealing a bouquet of wild flowers.

"Why, thank you." Phoenix hoped he wouldn't notice her blushing. He looked so sharp in his Prada shoes, black slacks, and peach dress shirt. "You don't look bad yourself."

They bounced compliments back and forth until Cahree had enough. "What about me? Don't I look pretty? J'all just completely forgot I was even in da room. Joo guys are too much."

Phoenix hugged her friend, "You look—"

"Very nice, too, Carmen." Caine finished Phoenix's sentence.

"Ooh, now joo finish each other's sentences, too? Dis is sickening." Cahree stuck her finger down her throat.

Phoenix put her flowers in a vase, and they were out.

THIRD ATTEMPT

Ever since the shooting in the Terrace, Rajii took it easy. He picked up the earnings from all spots, then laid low at Jamaira's crib.

Damn, these niggahs are getting crazy money! I see why they call themselves the Dough Boys. Rajii counted each bundle of money and wrote it in the ledger, making each lieutenant sign it. He didn't want any discrepancies. This was not required, but he knew that being the pickup man was just a test of honesty and trust.

After tallying up all earnings, Rajii realized he was sitting on a goldmine. Each time he opened the duffel bag, the palms of his hands itched. Holding over half a million, he turned around to watch his back. They gotta be tailing me. This much dough? Knowing I just betrayed my own peeps. Rajii looked around, but there was no one. Oh, these niggahs trying to test a brothah. Rajii planned on being loyal at least until he learned enough about the business. Rajii paged Blizz and put in his number, 187, as he pulled up at Bally's Fitness Center. Rajii grabbed the duffel bag from the backseat.

Blizz stopped pumping weights when he saw Rajii standing at the receptionist's desk, and walked over to him. "Thanks, man, I knew I left my gym bag in the backseat. Good looking. You wanna work out? I could get you a guest pass."

"Maybe next time," Rajii said, wondering where the money went from there. He still hadn't met his boss. He checked his watch. Shit, I'm gonna be late.

Rajii zipped through traffic and headed home. He was taking Jamaira out tonight. He'd arranged their date early in the evening. He didn't want Jamaira to think he was pushing up on her solely for the booty, and wanted to have her home before midnight.

Kye had told him about a spot where he wouldn't feel uncomfortable, looking over his shoulder every second. Captain's Galley was a shirt and tie atmosphere. Rajii bought himself a nice silk shirt and pair of brown dress slacks. He hadn't worn shoes since he was a young boy. He was definitely feeling himself. Kye gave him directions the night before. Rajii rode out to Captain's Galley afterwards. He wanted to impress Jamaira, and didn't want to get lost.

Rather than pulling into her lot and beeping his horn or chirping Jamaira, Rajii walked to her door and rang the bell.

"Hi, Jamaira. You ready?"

"Yes, I'm ready," Jamaira said, impressed by his appearance.

Rajii locked her arm under his and escorted her to his truck, opening the door for her. He remembered something Chase taught him. If you open the door for a girl and, once she's in, she doesn't lean over to unlock yours—she's a selfish bitch. As Rajii reached for the driver's side door handle, Jamaira leaned over and unlocked it. Just what he thought, she's a keeper.

On the way to dinner, Jamaira and Rajii engaged in smalltalk. She asked the basic questions: what kind of food

Eyes on the Pryze

he liked, what he liked about her, was he seeing anyone. Jamaira felt thankful that her mother and brother weren't home when Rajii arrived. She needed more time to decide if she should introduce him. Something was different about Rajii; he was nothing like the guys who tried to get with her. She still tried to feel him out.

They strolled the beach after dinner. Jamaira asked Rajii more personal questions. Just as he was about to share the horrid details of his life, a car rolled up beside them.

"Ay, bwoy, it nuh personal, strictly business." Nigel's trigger finger pushed out shots.

Rajii grabbed Jamaira and threw her to the sand, shielding her with his body. Too many witnesses to draw Nina. Screams came from everywhere, but Rajii only concerned himself with Jamaira's screams.

"Shop, I think I'm shot," Jamaira held a blood-soaked hand on her hip.

"Just be still," Rajii looked around and saw others lay wounded on the beach. "I'm dirty," he blurted out.

Jamaira understood. "Go! I'm alright. Go!"

Rajii dashed across the street to his truck. He heard sirens in the distance, but he couldn't leave her. He stashed Nina, then ran back to Jamaira's side.

"When they come over here, you don't know anything, okay?"

Jamaira nodded.

Rajii held her hand just until police arrived on the scene. He watched inconspicuously from across the street as she was placed into an ambulance. He didn't know who to call. Having never met her family, he hopped in his truck and called Kye.

"Yo, man, they tried that shit again! My girl got hit!" "Yo, man, you need me to come get you? You straight?" Just then, Rajii noticed he'd been shot. too, "Yo..." he fainted, not realizing it was just a graze.

Police stopped Nigel a few blocks from the scene. Nigel had tossed his gun along the road, but an officer retrieved it and continued in hot pursuit. Nigel immediately broke under pressure. After booking, they transported him to Bridgeport Mental Health.

Kye pulled up in a cab and saw Rajii's truck parked in the restaurant parking lot.

Rajii came too, but was still dazed. Slowly, he realized where he was, saw his cellphone at his feet, and heard Kye banging on the windshield.

"Yo, man, open the door. Shop, man, open the door!" Kye continuously yelled and banged on the windshield until Rajii made out the words and hit the auto lock.

"Ah, shit!" Rajii grabbed his arm as he fell into Kye. "Where's she? Where is she?"

"All I know is you called me and told me some cat was shooting and your girl got hit. I heard a lot of sirens. I figured you'd still be here, getting harassed by 5-O. So, I just jumped in a cab and came out here. You a'ight, man?"

Rajii looked around, trying to remember. Police still questioned people on the beach. Then Rajii noticed a white sheet laid over a body.

"Aw, man! Is she..." Rajii banged his hand on the steering wheel, "Ah!" pain shot up his arm.

Eyes on the Pryze

"Just chill, man, 'fore they come over here. I'll go see what's what. You don't want no one to place you at the scene."

Kye crossed the street and approached an officer. "I was talking to my wife on the phone, and I heard shots. She said she was hit then the phone went dead. Is she..." Kye stepped towards the body.

The officer stopped him. "Sir, I'm sorry, but you're going to have to step back. This is a crime scene."

"No, no! I want to know!"

"I'll check for you. Is she African-American?"

Kye nodded.

"Okay, son, you can calm down. This is an old White lady. Is that all you heard? Anything else you can tell me?"

"Yes, sir ... no, sir."

"Can I see some ID?" the officer pulled out a notepad.

Kye had to think quick. "Sorry, I jumped in a cab and came out here. I don't have no ID on me. Do you know where they may have taken someone who was shot?"

"Milford Hospital. Check there first," the officer said, walking away.

Kye returned to Rajii's truck, and told him what he'd learned. "Maybe you should take off that shirt before we head out," he pointed to the blood stains on Rajii's silk shirt.

Rajii reached into the backseat and retrieved a long sleeve black T-shirt. They then zipped to Milford Hospital.

***

The receptionist talked on the phone when they reached the information desk. Kye turned to Rajii and, in a whisper, asked his girl's name.

"Jamaira," Rajii whispered back.

I know Shop ain't fucking Blizz's sister. "Excuse me, I'm Jamaira's brother. I was told she was brought in with a gunshot wound."

"Last name?"

"Hutchinson, Jamaira Hutchinson."

The receptionist checked the records then pointed down the hall. "You can have a seat in the waiting area. I'll send the doctor to speak with you."

Rajii followed Kye, "Man, how did you know—"

Kye glared at Rajii. "Look, man, it's your life and you can live it any way you want, but you broke the Dough Boy code: Never mess with the next man's sister."

Rajii's mouth dropped. "Yo, man, I didn't know she was your sister. I would never disrespect our friendship. She never—"

Is this niggah fronting? He really don't know? "Not my sister. Blizz's sister."

Shit! "I didn't know. I've been seeing her for a minute, too. I ain't stunting on her, either. I really like her, man. What the fuck? Right before that bitch started shooting at me, she asked me where did I pop up from; what kind of lifestyle did I lead. I was about to tell her, then this shit happened. My word, son."

Kye believed him. Now Kye found himself caught between his friendship with Rajii and his loyalty to the Dough Boys. Fuck them Dough Boys. We vowed it was me and him. It ain't nothing but business with them boys.

Eyes on the Pryze

Rajii stared out the waiting room window, praying the doctor would come in and ease his worries.

"Uh, Mr. Hutchinson?"

Rajii stood and turned towards the voice. His worries began to subside until he noticed a police officer, not a doctor, stood in the doorway.

Damn! "Yes, I'm Mr. Hutchinson."

"I thought I'd find you here. I need to go over the statement you gave to one of the officers on scene."

Rajii nodded, although he knew he didn't give a statement.

"You stated that you were talking to your wife on the phone, then you heard shots and the phone went dead. Is that correct, sir?"

Kye winked at Rajii.

"Yes, officer," Rajii answered.

"Well, I'd hate to stir up ill-nature between you and your wife at a time like this, but other witnesses stated there was a young man with her when shots rang out."

"What the hell are you saying?"

The officer stepped back. "Well, sir, I'm not insinuating anything. I'm just going over the facts that were given to the officer on scene. Witnesses stated that after your wife was shot, the young man fled the scene. What I'm having a problem with is the young man's description. You match the description. Can you explain that?"

"Man, if you don't get this ... this ... pi ... cop out my face... I can't believe this shit. First he wants me to think that Jamaira's cheating on me, then he wants me to think she's cheating with me. Is this some crazy ass..." Rajii turned to Kye then back to the officer. "Look, son, my wife wasn't with anyone! You hear me? Why would I be talking to her while she's with another man? Answer that."

Kye was so caught up in Rajii's performance, he started to believe the shit himself. "Calm down, man. I don't think that's what the officer's saying. He's just doing his job."

"Exactly, sir. And your name?"

"Kye ... my name's Kye."

"Last name?"

Rajii came to Kye's rescue. "So what are you saying? Why all these questions? I don't know what the hell happened out there. All I know is Jamaira was shot and I still haven't been told anything."

The officer focused on Rajii again. "Well, sir, all I wanted to let you know is that the other witnesses stated that she wasn't alone. And, I needed to know if you knew the man she was allegedly with. Plus, no cell phone was recovered at the scene."

"Mr. Hutchinson," the doctor walked in, "Jamaira has been asking for you. At first, we thought she was saying 'shot,' that she'd been shot. But after calming her down, we realized she was saying 'Shop'. Are you Shop Hutchinson?"

Rajii nodded and noticed the officer taking notes. That didn't bother him because Shop Hutchinson didn't exist.

"Excuse me," the doctor took Shop into the hall to discuss Jamaira's condition. "Sir, your wife's going to be fine. She was hit twice. Once in her upper arm; we retrieved the bullet without any complications. The other bullet hit her right side, but went straight through. She's lost a lot of blood so she's weak, but very lucky. She'll be fine.

"I'd like to keep her a few days for monitoring; make certain her wounds don't become infected. Then she'll be able to go home. There's some paperwork you need to sign, then you can see her. She's in room 187."

Did he just say 187? This shit is bananas. But my baby's a'ight. That's all I care about.

The officer stepped out, requesting to speak with Mrs. Hutchinson.

"Well, officer, her husband hasn't even seen her yet. She's weak and needs her rest. I'm limiting her visits to family. Mrs. Hutchinson will be here a few days. You'll have to come back later."

Kye heard the conversation. Whew! Shop has more luck than a little bit.

"When she's up to it," Rajii began, "I'll have her call the precinct. Do you have a card?" Rajii read the card: Detective Shaahyid Matthews. "Look, Detective Matthews, I'm sorry about earlier. I was just worried about my wife."

"Yeah, you have her do that," the detective said, unconvinced by Rajii's performance. He then turned to Kye, "I didn't get your last name."

"I didn't give it to you." Kye walked off with Rajii.

Detective Matthews began to pursue Kye, then thought against it. In due time, he'll know everything. "You're right. You didn't." The detective then turned to leave the hospital, thinking, Who names their child Shop?

THE TRUTH

Rajii slowly opened the door to Jamaira's room. He found her asleep, and sat at her bedside until she woke.

"Shop? That you?"

Rajii stood and held her hand, "Yeah, ma, it's me."

Kye stood as well, to let Jamaira know that she and Rajii were not alone.

"Kye? What are you doing here?" Jamaira's eyes widened as she struggled to sit up. She became frantic, "Is Blizz here with you?" Her grasp tightened on Rajii's hand.

"Jamaira, calm down. The doctor said you need to rest." Kye walked towards her. She let go Rajii's hand as he came closer. Kye leaned over and kissed her forehead. "Hey, cuz."

Rajii backed away. "Cuz? Come on. Niggah, this is your cousin? When were you gonna tell me that?"

Kye sat on the edge of Jamaira's bed, "Man, when I told you about the code—"

"Code?" Jamaira interrupted, knowing all to well about the code. "What? You're down with the Dough Boys? Talk about holding shit back! When the hell were you gonna tell me that?"

"I think I'ma leave out so you and my man can talk," Kye stood and tried to give dap to his boy.

Rajii pushed his hand away, "Go ahead wit dat, man!"

Eyes on the Pryze

"Yo, man, it ain't like that. We're boys. Not because of the crew, but because we just are. I'll be right outside. We'll talk."

"Well" Jamaira folded her arms, "you have something to tell me? Explain."

Rajii came clean about everything, but told her he really had no idea she was Blizz's sister. "Now I got beef two ways. I betrayed my crew to join another, and unintentionally broke their code, too. Now I'm falling…"

Jamaira couldn't believe her ears. I know he wasn't about to say he loves me. I thought it was just me.

"Why didn't you tell me Blizz was your brother?"

"Shop, Blizz always intimidates my friends. He's been choosing who I talk to and where and when I go for the longest. I knew there was something about you that may have been different. I felt like you were your own person and that's what attracted me to you. Not the money, your car or anything materialistic. I hope I'm right. I really like you, Shop, and my feelings seem to grow each minute I'm with you. Whether you finish what you were saying or not, I can tell you feel the same way."

Rajii grinned. "Is that right? So you think you know me, huh?"

Jamaira pulled him close, "I do now."

Rajii nodded.

"What's up with you and Kye? He usually rolls alone. You and him seem tight. He's never cared about anyone since his road dawg was killed."

Rajii wondered why Kye never spoke of that; knew he still had a lot to learn about his boy. First, his intention was to use Kye to get info on the Dough Boy enterprise, but he took a genuine liking to Kye.

"Yeah, Kye's my man. I like his style. I need to talk to him. I want us to stay cool even if the rest of the crew questions my loyalty. If all else fails and I'm out, I'd like Kye to roll with me.

"As for your brother dictating who I see...shit, he needs to fall back. I got this."

Jamaira caressed his face. Just as she was about to lay her pretty lips on him, Kye burst in.

"Yo, man, we cool?"

Rajii didn't need to think about his answer. "For life, man!"

"Be ready for beef, man. Blizz just stepped to the nurse's station. He don't look too happy. Any way it goes down, I got you. That's my cuz and all, but me and you ... you know how it is."

A tear ran down Jamaira's cheek. She knew all too well that her brother had a way of changing niggahs' minds, even when they thought otherwise. "Remember I love you, Shop. No matter what my brother says."

"Same here, ma. Don't worry. I said I got this."

Blizz burst into the room, rushed at Rajii, pinning him against a wall.

"Niggah, I know you ain't put my baby sister in harm's way. Niggahs get dirt naps for that!"

"What? Fuck was I supposed to know she was your sister?"

Rajii grabbed Blizz's arms; Blizz had the size advantage. Blizz tossed him into a chair.

Eyes on the Pryze

"I knew you was a snake ass bitch from jump! But you fucking with an official Dough Boy now."

Rajii, stunned, wondered what he meant by official. Jamaira saw blood seep through Rajii's shirt and on to her brother's hands.

"Get the fuck off him! You're hurting him!" Jamaira screamed.

Blizz punched Rajii. Kye ran up on Blizz, throwing him to the floor. "Y'all both gonna get put out this bitch. That's what you want, Blizz? Huh? Let him talk."

"So what you saying? I ain't official!"

Shop, Rajii–what the fuck ever–has to go. "I'm calling Caine. You'll be put on trial for this shit. If he says you have to be cut off, it is what it is."

Kye knew if Caine gave Blizz the okay, Shop was a dead man. "You need to let the man talk. That's always how we do. And he goes before the crew first, then Caine." Kye knew he was now gambling with his own life, so he took it to the max. "Go ahead, Shop, finish."

"Niggah, your bitch ass wanna be gangsta? Don't tell me shit. I run the Dough Boys. You wanna take sides?"

"Well, this is about me!" Jamaira said, "I say let him talk."

Blizz could see his baby sister was growing weak from all the chaos. Infuriated, he pointed at Rajii. "Shoot, partner!"

"If you wanna be real, I never broke no code. I met Jamaira the day I made the drop to you. I stopped at the gas station before I came to you. You said I wasn't official. When we sat at the round table, then I was officially a Dough Boy. Now what?"

Felisha Bradshaw

"Is that true, Jamaira? And don't lie to me, you're in enough shit already."

"Yes, I met him at the gas station. So, he couldn't have known."

"Whatever. Who knows if your sneaky ass is telling the truth. You could be trying to save his bitch ass."

"What? You think I go around bragging about your ass! You ain't shit, Blizz. You betrayed me over and over again. Don't make me tell Kye what you're really about. As far as I'm concerned, you ain't nothing. Not even my brother. I hate your ass."

"What you got to tell me, Jamaira?" Kye piped up.

"Keep that shit to yourself, Jam." Blizz grabbed his sister's arm. Rajii jumped to his feet.

"You think you know me?" Jamaira challenged her brother.

"Keep that shit to yourself, Jam," Blizz repeated, yanking her arm and twisting it.

"What! You wanna put your fucking hands on me! Ooh, you done fucked up now. He had Shotz killed. It wasn't no drive-by. He did it, Kye. Blizz ordered the hit. He killed Shotz!"

The night Shotz was killed, Kye was clean. Without a piece on him, he couldn't come to his best friend's aid, and had to run for cover. Kye carried that guilt—and a piece—ever since.

Kye fell against the wall and slid down with his hands covering his face. He roared into his cupped hands, then reached under his pants leg and pulled out a nickel plated .25. In one quick breath, Kye rose to his feet and was on

Blizz. "I promised myself when I found the bitch who killed my boy, I would drop him where he stood."

"What on God's green earth is going on in here? This is a hospital, for Christ's sake. You two have to leave. Now. Mr. Hutchinson, spouse visiting hours end in twenty minutes."

"Fuck this! I don't need your ass. I don't need nobody ... and Shotz had it coming. He was a punk, anyway."

"You're a dead niggah! Fuck you and the Dough Boys. They had to know about this. Fuck y'all! I'll be in the lobby, Shop."

The rage in Kye's eyes made it clear to Blizz that wasn't a mere threat. *I truly slept that lil bitch!* Blizz escaped death—this time—but knew he had to take out Kye and Rajii before they took him out. That wasn't his only problem. He had to tell Caine what just went down.

Rajii sat with Jamaira until spouse visiting hours ended. After all the madness, he finally told her that a detective had questioned him and needed to speak with her as well. He handed Jamaira Detective Matthews card while making sure they got their story straight.

"You gotta call him. I don't think he's gonna let this go. The old White lady next to you died, so he ain't gonna let this shit ride. Some witnesses said they saw you walking with a guy matching my description. Just tell him some dude tried to talk to you, but you told him you were spoken for and that was that, okay?"

Rajii kissed Jamaira, promising her everything would be alright. And once it was, he had a surprise for her. He left and met up with Kye in the lobby.

"We better head back to my place. The Terrace is gonna be off-limits for a while. Blizz gotta go. Let's do this!"

Rajii had never brought anyone to his home. But Kye proved he wasn't just anyone. Kye nodded without saying a word. Rajii knew that learning who was behind his best friend's murder hit Kye hard.

**

"Yo, man, I didn't know none of this was going down! Rajii's seeing my sister. They claim they didn't know nothing about the other being connected to me. Since we put him on, there's been two shootouts ... that I know of."

"Yow tings fucked. Cha!" Caine had little patience for fuck-ups. "Cuz yuh wan run tings like a big mon. Why yuh nevah run dis to mi before?"

"Man, I didn't have the time. I was trying to research shit before I put it on you."

"Look, mon, dis need fixin and yuh gwan fix it. If mi lose mi connect wit boss, yuh gwan regret dis."

Blizz knew there was no way to sugarcoat this, so he just put it all out there. He even explained the kicker—the Kye situation.

On the other end, Caine tugged at his waistband in frustration. This was another trait he shared with his identical twin. "Yuh bettah turn dis round. Make dis enemy into bredren or deal wit mi, seen?" Caine hung up the phone. He knew he had to set things forward. There was no time for further mishaps.

IN SEARCH OF LOVE: Part Two

"Everything okay? Why are we in the park? Where's Phoenix?" Vina was anxious to talk to her friend. She wanted to be the first to introduce her to Phillie.

"She moved to the city all by herself? What would make her do something like that? The lady at the front desk said she's no longer there?"

Now Vina grew worried. "What do you mean not there? Moved?" Phillie held Vina's hand. "We'll never find her. This campus is huge!" Vina knew her friend would never live alone in New York. She must have a roommate ... but who?

"Well, I'm not giving up. I came here to get my girl back and I ain't leaving until I do!"

Chase told them they had to come up with a way to find her.

"You want to split up? Where do we start?" Phillie was familiar with the campus. In fact, a few of her friends still attended NYU.

"Well, it's getting late and classes don't start for two days. The lady gave me a map of the campus. Let's just chill for now. We can go back to the hotel, freshen up, and divide the map. Then we can take it from there." Vina threw her hands up in defeat.

Phillie wanted to give her hope; although, she had little hope herself. "I'll hit up a few friends that still go here and see what they know. Got a picture of her?"

Vina hugged Phillie, "That's a great idea. You know, you never cease to amaze me!"

Chase opened his wallet and pulled out Phoenix's prom picture. "Never leave home without it!" He handed the picture to Phillie. "Don't lose it! Come on, let's enjoy the city. We got mad shit to do in a few days."

A horse-drawn carriage approached. Phillie looked at Vina and smiled. Phillie waved down the man steering the horse.

"Your buggy has arrived, my princess."

Vina giggled. "Why thank you, my prince." She wasn't sure if calling Phillie a prince would offend her. Little did she know she made Phillie feel like a king. *This is what life is supposed to be about. Even if my mother wouldn't approve of this lifestyle, I know she'd be happy just because I'm living.* She snuggled with Phillie.

"Guess I'll take a cab," Chase said as the carriage pulled off.

Just across the street, Phoenix walked hand-in-hand with her new man, with Cahree in tow.

"Can we get an iced espresso?" Cahree got Phoenix hooked on them.

"Anyting fi yuh," Caine held the door for them.

"Wait!" Vina yelled, pointing toward the café. "I think I just saw Phoenix with Chase." Then she remembered what Chase was wearing. "Never mind. That guy was dressed up, but it sure looked like them. Anyway, Chase would've called if he found her so soon. Now I'm seeing shit. I can't wait to find her."

Vina and Phillie arrived back at the hotel; the doorman helped both out of the buggy.

Chase couldn't wait for Phillie and Vina to return. Being alone with his thoughts was driving him crazy. He kept imagining the worst: Phoenix mugged in some alley, or laying in a bush in Central Park. "Ugh, Phoenix, where are you!"

In the adjoining room, Vina heard him scream. She rushed into Chase's room. "Chase?...Chase, you a'ight?" He wasn't in the living area. She tapped on his bedroom door. "Chase? You okay? I heard a scream."

"Just frustrated, V. What if she's hurt or needs my help?"

Vina threw her hands on her hips. "Boy! You scared the shit out of me! You know Phoenix...she's a tough one." Vina shared Chase's concerns, then dismissed them. "Plus, I know she had to call her mom with her new address. They wouldn't have approved if they thought she wouldn't be safe. I wish I could tell her mom why she's not talking to us, and what happened to me. Maybe then she'd tell us where she's at."

"Well, let's use the resources we have first. If nothing turns up, that might be our last resort. How was your carriage ride?"

Vina became starry eyed.

"Never mind. I know that look. Yo, niggahs are really gonna be hating on Phillie when we get back."

V was never one to care about what people said, but knew this would be the talk of the town. She'd be put on blast. But, like Chase said, they'll be haters.

Phillie stuck her head in, "I'ma be out for about an hour. I got something to take care of."

Phillie walked to Christopher Street. She looked at the storefront that she planned to open. For Sale. She still awaited a reply from the loan officer. She'd saved just about every dime she made from slinging rock. Her account was fat, but not enough to open her dream bar/restaurant. Her mother was the only person who knew she was pursuing her dream. She had yet to tell Vina of her plans, but would in due time. She didn't want Vina to think she was looking for a handout. The biggest issue was the commute. Phillie put her face to the window. She loved the brick walls and the natural wood floors. Soon...very soon! On her way back, she stopped at a toy shop and bought a surprise for Vina.

***

Phoenix, Cahree, and Caine tried to decide which club to attend. Cahree didn't care, as long as the grown and sexy were going to be there. She had her fake ID ready. As long as Phoenix was stepping out with Caine, she was open to anything.

"Alright, mi love de 40/40 Club. Mi bredren is givin a private bash," Caine said.

Phoenix was ecstatic. She pulled Cahree close, squeezing her arm. "Oh, my God! That's the club Jay-Z owns."

Eyes on the Pryze

Cahree couldn't care less, "Jay-Z, P. Diddy, R. Kelly ... I just wanna meet my Denzel."

The 40/40 Club's line extended around the corner. Caine walked up to the head of the line. The bouncer gave him a bear hug.

"Ain't seen you in a minute, bossman! How's it going?"

"Nuttin, mon. Just out wit mi 'oman."

The bouncer looked over Caine's shoulder. "Nice, man, either way you good." He let Caine's party in. "Have a good time!"

The stools at the bar were padded with soft brown leather. Flat screen televisions were mounted on steel poles; additional steel poles suspended lounge chairs from the ceiling. Not far from the bar, cream leather chairs sat side-by-side facing a wall of brown suede seating. Cahree was nowhere to be found. As soon as they entered the club, she went on her way. Caine made sure Cahree was not served any alcoholic beverages. He then introduced Phoenix to a few hip hop celebrities as well as professional athletes. Phoenix was amazed by how many people Caine knew. They were amongst the elite, and she was loving it. Every now and then, someone would come up to Caine and compliment him on a job well done. Before heading up to the Cognac VIP room, they stopped at the far side of the bar where Caine handed P a drink.

"Thanks." She took a sip. *A virgin Martini? I guess I have to respect that.*

Cahree approached P. "Look, another Denzel," then took off again.

Phoenix was glad that Cahree wasn't the type of girl who needed her constant companionship.

Felisha Bradshaw

A gentlemen dressed in an Armani suit came over to Caine. He gave him his business card and a page from a magazine. "I need this done before October. Can it be done?" Caine looked at the page and nodded. "Great. I look forward to speaking with you. How about this week sometime?" Caine never uttered a word; all he did was nod.

"Who's that?" Phoenix asked. "He looks important."

"'im no important. 'im check fi mi, not mi check fi him."

"You didn't have to get an attitude. You seem to know a lot of wealthy people. What is it you do for a living?"

Caine's face softened. "Oh. In mi business, mi make tings like dis." He showed Phoenix the magazine page. "It's a tree level deck fi 'im yard."

"Oh, so you're a carpenter."

He smiled. "True, but mi own de business. Mi 'ave tree companies. Let's go get Cahree. We go to de VIP room. Come."

That night, they partied and danced till the sun came up. Caine teaching her how to wind was what Phoenix remembered most. His body gyrating on her made her moist between the legs. Feeling his body so close to hers made her want to melt inside him.

"I'm starving. We going to breakfast?" Cahree danced the night away, yet still had energy.

Caine nodded.

Chase decided to stay behind. His mind was so fixated on Phoenix, he knew he wouldn't be much company.

That was fine with Phillie, who wanted to take Vina to Lover Girls; a lesbian club.

I never seen so many lesbians in my life. Vina didn't want to come off as naïve but, every now and then, she'd slyly point to people in the crowd.

"Yup, that's a girl." Phillie enjoyed opening Vina's mind to a lifestyle she was now part of.

"Ooh, shit, this ain't nothing like the clubs back home. I love New York. I don't care if we never leave ... but I wanna find Phoenix."

Vina pushed Phillie to the wall, and began grinding her shapely body up and down in front of Phillie. Phillie was about to cream all over herself. The attraction she felt for Vina mixed with love and the drinks she'd consumed ... Phillie was euphoric.

The lights flickered signaling last call.

"I'll be right back, a'ight?"

Vina nodded. Phillie had to get away for a second, plus she saw an old friend of hers. "What's good, Lex?"

Lex turned around. "Yo! Phil, what's up? Ain't seen you in a minute." Lex introduced Phillie to her new girl, a Chinese chick.

"You still at NYU?" Phillie asked. Lex nodded. "I need to talk to you about somebody I need to find."

Lex excused herself. "You know if I can help you, I will. What's up?"

Phillie gave Lex a synopsis.

"Let's talk over breakfast. You alone?"

Phillie pointed to Vina on the other side of the club; looking so sexy winding her hips and sipping her drink.

"Damn! That's you?" Phillie smiled and nodded. "Where y'all staying? I can put you up, you know? Like the old days."

"Nah. We're straight. We're staying at Hotel Chelsea."

Lex stepped back. "What? Doing it big, huh? Let me find out. You still doing the cooking thing?"

"Yeah. I'm about to do something that you may want to get with. We'll talk. Just not around the wifey." Phillie walked Vina over to Lex and her girl. They introduced themselves then piled in Vina's truck.

Lex's cell phone vibrated.

"What's good? ... Nah. You'll never guess who I'm with. ... Nah. ...Phil...wait," Lex covered the mouthpiece. "You wanna stop by the 40/40 to pick up Syncere?"

Phillie nodded. "Tell that bitch we're even now!"

They whipped around to the 40/40 club and waited for Syncere, a bartender in the VIP rooms.

"I know Syncere loves this job. She knows she a celebrity trick!" Lex laughed.

"I know that's right."

Vina turned to Phillie. "Is she gay? Femme or like you?"

"Yeah, sort of like me. She don't think so, though. She swears she's a real man. You'll see."

They waited fifteen minutes. Then, what looked like a small framed young man approached the truck.

"What? Phil rolling like this!" Her swagger was masculine, and she grabbed her crotch when she talked.

Vina's mouth dropped. She even thought she saw a hint of a mustache.

"See, I told you." Phillie jumped out of the truck to hug her old friend. Phillie was a lot larger than Syncere. Her hug lifted Syncere off the ground.

"A'ight, a'ight. Can we eat?" Lex interrupted their reunion.

Syncere jumped in the back, and the introduction thing started again. Phillie asked who she bartended for tonight.

"Some weak ass Jamaican dude. You know the one that can't stop hating on me?"

"Who?" asked Phillie.

"He sings that song "Bossman"? He's got raggedy, thin dreads."

"You mean, Beenie Man? I love his music, but he definitely has some issues."

Syncere looked at Lex. Lex whispered, "V's new to the game. She'll learn."

During breakfast, Phillie showed Chase and Phoenix's prom picture to Lex.

"Damn, she's fine. I'd like to find her ass myself. I haven't seen a new face like that on campus. But when I do, I will definitely hook you up with the 411. You got another picture, so I can send it to my ace? His ass is the eyes and ears of NYU. If she gets hated on too much, he'll know. Anything that has to do with his bitch ass gossiping, I can find out."

Vina sifted through her pocketbook. "Here. I have one. I didn't want to give it up. But I guess if it finds Phoenix, I'm down."

Phillie passed the picture through Syncere. She looked at it before passing it along. "I saw this chick at the club."

"You sure?"

"Yeah, that's her. She was a nice lady. That's the girl that was with the dread. He's a frequent customer at the 40/40. Gets mad props. Big tipper, too."

"With a Jamaican guy? This girl right here? You're positive it was her?"

Phillie retrieved the photo she'd given Lex. "Dread, as in this guy?"

"What's up with you two? Yeah, that's him. They call him Caine. I don't know if it's his real name."

Vina was glad Chase found her, but a bit upset he didn't call to tell them. "You mean Chase?"

"Caine, Chase, something like that. But I do think they called him Caine."

Phillie turned to Vina. "I didn't know Chase hung out in the city like that."

Vina called Chase. "Call us. That's fucked up you didn't let us know you found her. I guess y'all are busy. Well, when you two finish, call me."

RAJII

Rajii entered the code to gain access to his residence within the gated community. He found a vacant spot in the visitors' parking area. Rajii never parked in the same spot twice, and keeping a mental note of frequent visitors made him feel secure.

The ride had been quiet. Rajii didn't intrude on Kye's thoughts, and figured Kye would open up to him when ready. They arrived at Rajii's residence, ending a business day earlier than usual, but this day had been exhausting.

"You can stay in my spare room. It's never been slept in." Rajii plopped beside Kye on the living room couch.

"You know, Shop, I knew that you were just using me that day we ate at Drumstick. What I don't know is why." Kye caught Rajii off guard. "Go ahead, man! If we're going to be boys like that then you need to fill me in on shit! Feel me?"

"Kye ... shit is foul, real foul right now. I don't think it's the time for that." Rajii attempted to stand, but Kye held him down.

"Serious, man. Right now my life is in your hands; just as yours is in mine. I need to know that when shit goes down, I have a true friend and soldier behind me."

"Yo, man, if you only knew what I was thinking when all this shit went down. I've been a selfish muthafuckah. I betrayed my boy. You know, that niggah brought me out of the worst shit. I was eating maybe twice a week back then. My moms ain't right. She's on that shit. Chase...he...he... man...I can't believe I did all that for this." Rajii pulled out his keys and started kicking the ottoman in front of him. "He was like a big brother to me. He showed me how to grind; put me on—just like that. I went from a street corner niggah to being trusted with the earnings from his spots. But, nah, my ass wanted more. So when Blizz approached me on some get down or lay down, I said fuck it. Can you believe it went down just like that? I made a decision just like that, on the spot. Just to get down. I didn't even think why he chose me until it was a done deal; or how he knew I picked up the stash for the 357. When he told me I'd be getting ten G's a week, that;s all I wanted to hear. I didn't even think that, when he asked me for the earnings, I was probably getting paid out of it."

Kye shifted in his seat; couldn't believe what he was hearing. He tried to put himself in Rajii's shoes, but Blizz paying Rajii, a new hustler, ten G's was too much for him to overlook. "Niggah, did you say ten G's a week? I don't give a fuck if it's Dough Boys' money or not. I get paid the most cause I put in the work. I got over five bodies and I get five G's, sometimes four. Yeah, that niggah has a plan for your ass. That's okay, cause it won't go down. He's a dead man!"

There goes that twitch. Rajii didn't know if he should continue.

"Man, I could kill that bitch with my bare hands."

"Come on, man. You got that monster face and you're hyped, and you expect me to tell you this shit? You know I've seen you in action."

Eyes on the Pryze

"Sorry. Go ahead, man."

Rajii watched the fire in Kye's eyes die down, but he wasn't taking any chances. "Kye, man, where's your shit? Put all your warfare on the table."

"You, too, niggah." Kye laughed.

"A'ight, then, where was I? I wasn't about to give it all up, so kept about thirty percent of the money for myself—just in case I needed to bounce." Rajii pulled out his wallet. "This was me before. I used to drive a low rider RX7."

Kye laughed. "Man, you look like a baby in this shot." He looked at the young boy in the picture then at the Rajii who now sat next to him. "Yo, that shit don't even look like you! When did you take this pic?"

"Just a few weeks before I got down."

Kye had to respect his gangsta.

"Before I came to make the drop off to meet y'all boss, I met Jamaira. Got that number, and been seeing her ever since ... but you know that part. But when I handed over the dough, Blizz met me. I wanted to know who was the real head niggah in charge. So, when I scoped out how niggahs was eying you, I knew you were the man to see. I definitely slept your sneaky, beastie ass. On the ride, I was trying to get some info on the crew—how they operated—and thought in the midst of it all that you would school me on the bossman. Then when that shit went down and you went all out for me, it was clear that I found a niggah that I could respect. You really fucked me up with the shit you housed off Mike."

"So you knew that niggah?"

"Yeah. He's one of the Heavy Hitters in the 357. I know now they got a bounty on my head."

Felisha Bradshaw

After taking in Rajii's story, Kye decided to let bygones be bygones. As long as Rajii respected the rule: no secrets between boys, he was going to ride it out.

"Man, shit ain't changed. Except one thing. We ain't rolling with those niggahs anymore. It's just me and you, son! How much dough did you get from 357?"

Rajii went to the back room. He returned and poured a bag out in front of Kye.

"Damn! Y'all getting dough like that? That's at least a hundred G's."

"Nah, a rough eighty, eighty-five G's. You gotta remember it was after the first of the month. Normally, our spot pulls in about seventy-five to a hundred G's a piece. The spots I pick up from are only Fifth Street, what goes on at the local clubs: Side Effect and Novella's. It's short because I've been spending my change. I bought my truck; this place, you know? Why?"

"Check this."

WHATCHOO MEAN?

Phillie made sure each of her friends had her cell number, Vina's number, as well as the hotel's. "I'ma get up with y'all before we leave. No doubt."

Syncere exited the truck first. "Nice meeting you, ma!"

Lex and her girl exited the truck at the next stop. "See you next week, Phil. You, too, V." Lex turned around before heading in her place. "You a'ight, ma! Even if you are a newbie."

Vina laughed. She and Phillie headed back to hotel; still no word from Chase.

"Phillie, thanks for looking out. I know you didn't have to try so hard to help find Phoenix, but I'm glad you did; and I love you for it." Phillie helped her out of the truck and passed the keys to the doorman.

"Baby, I don't think you understand. I'd do anything for you. Not just because I love you, because I do, but because you deserve it. Let's go get some sleep."

Vina had other things in mind. She couldn't get to the room fast enough. They didn't bother to check on Chase. It was still early, plus they wanted to be together.

Phillie ran Vina a warm bath. Vina switched things up. She invited Phillie in the tub, instead of having her sit on the edge like she normally would.

"I wanna bathe you for a change. I want this night to be about Phillie."

Damn she's sexy. Phillie noted how the bubbles hid just enough to make her desire Vina more. One touch from Vina's hand and Phillie was hooked for life.

Chase sat up most of the night. He couldn't sleep with all the night terrors he continuously experienced. He knew Phoenix was in trouble; could feel it. He called Cutty.

"Wha'um? Bout time mi reach yuh. Whatta gwan wit tings?"

"De block is 'ot. Mike ... 'im dead an' boss tek way Nigel! ... Yow! Yuh dere?"

"Ya, mon, ... what 'appen?"

"Mi nevah know bout Nigel till today. It pon de news; inna de papah. 'im nevah know bout the bounty."

"Bounty? Whey yuh chat bout bounty?"

Cutty hesitated. "Mi put a bounty pon 'is 'ead. Tings was gettin tight. Twenty G's to catch a teef."

Chase slammed his hand on the nightstand. "So...yuh run tings, eh? Ah yuh who mek tings 'ot. Twenty G's mek a man do anyting...yuh nevah know? Cha! Now one of mi soldiers dead and boss got de udder! Yuh bettah find Raj and mek dis disappear, seen?" Chase hung up.

Cutty never got the opportunity to tell Chase that Nigel's old girl Tyeshia gave him a lead on Rajii's girl's address, and he was on it as they spoke.

Mi a big man, seen? 'e cyan chat to mi so! Cutty hissed his teeth. Things were going to change when this shit was over. He was getting too old to let a youth tell him what to do. 'im wit de fuckery. Mi mek all dis 'appen ... mi oversee

Eyes on the Pryze

de runnings ... mi bust de shots ... mi! Cutty was furious. He did owe Chase at one time, but he paid that debt long ago. He was ready to take his savings and head back home to Jamaica. 'oman like poison! Dat Yankee 'ave 'im by 'is seed. Nevah mi.

Cutty sat in his rental and waited. If dis gal no come soon.

Just then, an officer pulled up in front of the address Tyeshia had given him. He knocked on the door and a small framed woman answered. They spoke as the officer wrote something in his notepad, tipped his hat then walked away. Yes, bossman, mi too. Cutty followed Detective Matthews. He knew it would lead him to the girl ... Jamaira.

***

"Jam, what's going on with you and your brother? He mumbled something about you betraying him ... what's going on? I hate that I work so much. You and your brother used to be so close. We all were." Jamaira's mother started to cry. "If I was home more, you wouldn't be lying in that hospital now."

"Ma, Blizz is so busy in the streets, he can't see pass the money. And, for the record, me and you are close. I love you, Ma. I know you work hard to keep things together for all of us. If Blizz was any kind of son, he would be taking care of you, so you didn't have to work so hard."

Mrs. Hutchinson didn't know what her son really did for a living. She thought he worked two jobs to pay for Jamaira's school.

Felisha Bradshaw

"Ma, do you really think Blizz could afford a Mercedes Benz? You're still taking the bus to work. Think about it. I'm not going to say more over the phone, but just think about what I am saying to you. I gotta go, Ma."

Mrs. Hutchinson knew something wasn't right, but refused to believe what she suspected all along. She went into her son's room for the first time in a long while and searched for the answers to her questions.

***

"Excuse me, Mrs. Hutchinson, you have a visitor."

Damn! I don't need this right now!

Detective Mathews stepped into Jamaira's room. "Hi, Jamaira. I hope you're up to a quick visit. I'm Detective Mathews. I'm investigating the shooting. I just wanted to get your version of the incident."

Jamaira offered him a seat. "Sure. Not much I can tell. It happened so fast. How's the woman that was shot? Is she okay? I think the bullet hit her first then more shots came after."

"Sorry to say, but she died on the scene. What else do you remember?"

Jamaira carefully told her rehearsed version of the drive-by. "I usually take one night out the week to eat out, to get away from school and all. So I decided to go out to eat ... sometimes I take in a movie—"

"I understand that you weren't alone. Witnesses saw you with a gentleman on the beach."

Eyes on the Pryze

"Yeah, some buster was all up in my face. I told him I was taken, but he was determined. So I called my man to prove to him that I wasn't interested."

"Look, Jamaira, I know you dined with a man. African American; about five-seven. The waiter said you two were very much into each other. You even left with him, so let's not bullshit each other. I'm gonna get straight to the point. I know you weren't alone. If you were cheating on your so-called husband, just say so. This will go on the record but, unless there's something that doesn't add up, your so-called husband won't have to know. So, you want to rephrase your story?"

Jamaira poured on the tears. She even amazed herself.

"I'm sorry I lied to you. I was with someone, but I can't say who. He could lose everything. I could get in a lot of trouble. Maybe even expelled.

"I know you think I'm young and that I shouldn't protect him, but I pursued him. I love him, sir, and I don't want him to get into any trouble because of me. And the gentleman who I spoke with on the phone, the one who came to my aid, is not my husband. I'm not married, but I am engaged." Jamaira showed him the ring. "I love him, too. This is so crazy. Who would think I would be in the middle of a shootout, and all this would come out?"

Detective Matthews offered his handkerchief. "It's okay, Jamaira, but I do need to know his name."

Jamaira looked up from the handkerchief. "I'm sorry, I can't...I can't take a chance in anyone finding out. Promise me that it will only be used in the report. Please?"

"Can you at least tell me your fiancé's name?"

"Shop Harriston."

Felisha Bradshaw

"Your name is Jamaira, isn't it?"

"Yes. Jamaira Hutchinson."

"Here's your medical card. Your mom sent it to you. I promised I would give it to you."

Jamaira was glad she didn't give him a fake name. Satisfied with Jamaira's story, Detective Matthews left. He ruled her out as a suspect. These young girls are so naïve these days. I hope everything works out for her. He was back to square one. To hell with it. My replacement will have to sort this one out. Big Apple, here I come!

Cutty waited for the officer to leave the room before he made his move.

Jamaira picked up the phone.

"The detective came here. I told him what happened, but he didn't believe me. So, I had to come up with something quick. But I know he believed me when he left. He even gave me his handkerchief." Jamaira gave Shop the full rundown of her award winning performance.

"Thanks, ma. You're still my wife to me. When you coming home?"

"I'll know in a few. The doctor was in earlier and then the cop came. I'm waiting to find out now."

He instructed her to take a cab straight to his house. He wouldn't be able to see her otherwise.

"Make sure you're not followed. Have you seen your brother?"

"Nah. I think he's been getting drunk or high off that dust. My mom said he came in the house mumbling about me dissing him."

Eyes on the Pryze

Rajii liked that Blizz wasn't on his P's and Q's. That made their plan to off him easier. Rajii gave Jamaira the code to get in the gate and into the building.

"Whatever you do, don't write it down. Memorize it."

Cutty was just about to slip into Jamaira's room from across the hall. He pulled his ratchet knife from his pants leg, and took a few looks in both directions. Cha!

Jamaira's doctor exited a patient's room and was making rounds to hers. "Mrs. Hutchinson, you're free to go home. I just need to finish up your discharge papers. You can follow-up with your own physician."

Yes! Jamaira called Shop, slipped on her clothes then called a cab. A nurse wheeled her out, and she was on her way to see her man. Cutty tailed her.

Once she stepped in the first gate, Jamaira looked behind her, seeing no one. Cutty had parked his car at the edge of the gate, and slipped in before the gates closed.

Dis cyant be Rajji's yard. Cutty watched Jamaira enter the code to get into the building. She pushed open the door and Cutty grabbed her from behind. Jamaira tried to scream for help until she felt a knife at her throat. She winced as it pierced her skin. "No mek nuh sound or yuh dead. Mi nah wan hurt yuh, but if dat is your will so be dat, seen? Now listen and let mi mek dis clear."

Jamaira cried on the inside. She thought she wasn't followed. Shop, I'm sorry.

"Jus knock pon de door. If 'im say who, yuh answer dat it's yuh, seen?"

Jamaira nodded.

TURNING TABLES

Rajii had just gotten out of the tub, and awaited Jamaira's visit. He looked on the table and noticed the guns were still out. He tucked Nina in the couch then called Kye to come get his. He didn't want Jamaira to be reminded of the shooting.

"Did she leave yet?" Kye was making himself at home. He had a towel wrapped around his waist and wore Rajii's Nike slippers.

"Look at your ass; all comfy and shit."

Kye couldn't complain. Rajii was living right. After his baby mother moved away, he kept her apartment in the Terrace. He wanted to be close to Shotz's son to make sure he was taken care of. "Man, I could live up in here forever. Feel me? I didn't even know this shit was up here, and it's close to the Terrace, too. Shit, I need to get me one of these joints."

"Yo, Kye ... you know my shit is your shit. We can stay here together. I got two bedrooms. We can do this."

"I might as well. My baby mother's lease is up in about a month. If she ain't here to renew it, I'm gonna have to find a place anyway." Kye checked his watch. "When did Jamaira leave?"

Rajii checked his watch as well. "About twenty minutes ago. She should be here any minute."

Eyes on the Pryze

Kye grabbed his gun from the table. "Let me get my shit outta here, so you and your girl can be alone." Kye started to leave the room then he turned around and said, "thanks, man!"

Jamaira thought about knocking on a random door, but knew this mad man would surely kill the people who opened the door. She had to figure out a way to warn Rajii.

She knocked lightly when they reached his door.

"Who?"

Jamaira thought quickly. She mumbled a few words.

Cutty slowly took his hands off of her mouth. "No fuck wit mi nah!"

Jamaira lied and told him Rajii was going to be suspicious because she had a key.

"So why yuh knock?"

"You told me to."

"Didden mi say no romp wit mi, gal? Cut de fuckery and mek 'im see dat yuh locked out!"

"Who?" Rajii asked again, unsure of what was mumbled.

"Jam. I left my keys at the hospital."

She ain't got no keys. Oh, shit!

"A'ight, here I come."

Rajii ran to warn Kye. He then opened the door and reached out to hug Jamaira—and there was Cutty—standing behind her with his gun in one hand and the other holding a knife at Jamaira's throat. Rajii backed away.

"Cutty! Man, don't hurt her. She's pregnant." Rajii knew him all too well. He knew Cutty would never harm her if she was carrying a seed.

"No mek mi haf to, Raj. Back up and sit pon de sofa." Rajii sat. Cutty released Jamaira. "Yuh, sit dere!"

Kye attached the silencer to his piece, waiting to make his move. He'd heard the stories about 357's right-hand man, and he knew what he was up against. Let that niggah even flinch and his dreads will be splattered all over these walls.

"Rajii, yuh mek de wrong choice to fuck Chase. Mi cyant believe yuh bite de 'and…yuh know wha' dat mean, seen?"

Kye pointed the gun to the back of Cutty's head, "Nah, man, what the fuck does that mean?"

Un-fazed by the gun in his dreads, Cutty kept talking. "Bwoy, yuh no know who dis?"

Kye laughed. "I don't give a fuck bout you, Cutty. You need to be worrying about who the fuck I am. You make one more move and you're one dead dread, seen, star?" Kye's been wanting to say that shit ever since he saw Marked for Death.

Cutty back-kicked Kye, sending him to the floor—but not before Kye let off a shot.

The bullet skinned the side of Cutty's head. Before Cutty could let off a shot, Rajii jumped up and hit Cutty in the back of the head with the butt of his gun, knocking Cutty out.

Rajii searched Cutty, retrieving two more pistols and his infamous ratchet knife. "I told you Cutty was old school. You just had to do that old movie shit. One more down and we're even."

Kye, still in shock, just knew he was a dead man. No one has ever caught him sleeping since Shotz was killed. "Yo, man, on some real shit … we even."

Eyes on the Pryze

    Cutty started moaning and Rajii hit him again, twice as hard.
    "Yo, I got some rope in that closet. Tie this niggah up. We don't want his ass to be able to move."
    Kye looked at Rajii strangely. "Yo, man, let me find out you into that freaky shit."
    "Man, stop playing. I used it to tie my mattresses to the roof of my truck."
    Jamaira was still dazed. "I did what you said. I checked to see if I was being—"
    Rajii walked over to her. "Ma, I know, I know. It's okay. Go in the kitchen and get you something to drink, okay? Let me and Kye handle this."
    Kye tied Cutty up like he was a boy scout and dragged him into the master bathroom.
    "What we gonna do with him?"
    Cutty came to. "Yow, bwoy!"
    Kye kicked Cutty in the gut. "That's for putting your feet on me. What's up with Jamaicans and kicking?"
    Cutty was getting too old for this. He wouldn't be able to endure what Kye wanted to give him. Rajii had Cutty's cell phone. He saw numerous messages from Chase's cell phone.
    "When's the last time you talked to Chase?" Rajii stood away from Cutty. He wasn't taking any chances.
    Cutty spat towards Rajii's feet. "Fuck yuh! Mi nevah betray mi bwoy! Mi tek it to Jah!"
    Rajii knew he meant every word, but Kye wanted to torture him for the information they needed. "Man, let me get at this muthafuckah. I saw some shit on Lethal Weapon that'll make his old ass talk."

Cutty laughed at Kye. "Yuh fool, seen?" He then looked at Rajii. "Yo, mon, yuh deal wit fool?"

"Man, stop playing. What's up with you and the movie shit? Let's bag this niggah up. Let him breathe in his own death. I got a plan." Rajii and Kye put on gloves before bagging up Cutty in an industrial garbage bag.

"Jamaira, where did Cutty get to you?"

"I was already inside the first gate. When I got to the door to punch in the numbers, he came up from behind. Why? Where's he at?"

Kye dragged Cutty into the living room.

"Y'all got him in that? Is he dead?"

Kye grinned with a crazed look in his eyes. "If he ain't, he soon will be." Kye began jumping in place.

Jamaira worried about him. He'd always been a low key, calm guy.

"Kye, you a'ight?"

"Cuz, I'm good. You okay?" Kye pointed to the dried line of blood on her neck.

"Oh!" Jamaira touched the thin cut. "Yeah, I'm okay ... it feels like a paper cut."

"Kye, go and get dressed. Wear dark colors ... you're about my size. Look in the closet next to your room. I'ma figure out how we're going to get this garbage outta here without looking suspicious." Rajii remembered the set of keys he took out of Cutty's pocket. 'Yo, bet the stash house keys are on that ring. He never went anywhere without a set." Still wearing gloves, Rajii grabbed a small trash bag and bagged Cutty's guns, knife, and keys. *That's all I'd need is for this shit to get traced back to me.*

Kye returned dressed in all black.

"Yo, man, why the fuck you got my Timberland brush and polish?"

"I need this, man, for camouflage. As light as I am, my face will stick out like a White boy at the Million Man March."

"Man, put that shit down! We're definitely gonna talk when this is over." Rajii didn't want to leave Kye alone with the body. He turned to Jamaira, "Keep him busy."

Rajii went to Kye's room. The window facing the woods was wide open. Rajii sniffed the air. *I knew that niggah was acting strange. He done found my stash. He don't even look like the kind that can handle this shit.* Rajii sealed the bag and placed it back in his spot. *I know not to smoke around his ass ... he all silly and shit.* Rajii looked out the window. He figured if they could get the body out that window, they'd be straight.

He dressed and returned to the living room. He looked at Kye then glanced at Jamaira. She threw up her hands.

"We were talking about back when we were kids and—"

Kye was knocked out. Rajii shook his head, "Damn! Now I got to do this shit myself." He let Kye sleep off his high. He knew he'd need him later when he got to the drop-off spot, and wanted Kye to have a clear head.

"I can help you. I know you didn't want to leave Kye alone, but it doesn't look like he'll be waking up for a minute." Jamaira pushed Kye over. "See?"

Rajii stared at the bag that held Cutty's body. For a second, his conscience kicked in. Jamaira sensed that things were beginning to take a toll on her man. "I know, baby, but you had to do it. I was freaked out, too, but then I said it was either him or you or us." She was definitely a ride to die chick. She held him close and whispered, "When this is all done and we have some us-time, I want to share my love with you. I, I never been with anyone before."

Rajii stepped back. "Never?"

Jamaira confirmed.

"Never!" That got his adrenalin going. Rajii kicked the bag. Cutty didn't respond. He kicked it a few more times just to make sure. Still no response. "Grab that end."

They carried the body to the bedroom window.

"What's that smell?"

Rajii explained.

"He doesn't even smoke." Jamaira shook her head.

"That haze will do it every time." Rajii refocused on the situation at hand. "We're going to have to wait a few hours before we get him outta here. Most people in the building work 9-5's. They sleep early and wake up early. I want to make sure no one sees us drop him."

They returned to the living room to check on Kye; still sleeping. Jamaira called home from Kye's phone.

"Hi, Mom, I'm okay; I'm with Kye. He picked me up and we're going out to eat. That hospital food was garbage."

"Your brother's taking the argument between the two of you real bad. I know now Blizz is up to no good, but he's still your brother."

Jamaira promised her mother she would call then hung up. She hated lying to her mother.

AIN'T NO WAY!

After a few hours of sleep, Vina jumped to her feet. She couldn't wait to see Phoenix. She rehearsed over and over again in her head what she was going to say to her.

"Phillie, get up! I want you to be there when I tell Phoenix about us. Phillie! Phillie!"

Phillie grabbed Vina and pinned her down. "Girl, if you don't take your butt back to sleep." Phillie buried her head under the pillows.

"Come on! You promised."

Phillie promised a lot of things last night. The way Vina was putting it on her, who wouldn't have promised her the world? "Okay, okay."

Vina called Chase. "I know you got my message. Don't try and play me."

"What? What are you talking about?"

"Let me speak to Phoenix."

"That shit ain't funny, V. You know how I feel about games." Chase hung up the phone.

Vina couldn't believe his selfishness. "You know he's trying to act like he ain't got a clue what I'm talking about? This shit ain't even funny."

Phillie followed Vina into Chase's room. Chase sat at the dining room table eating breakfast. No sign of Phoenix anywhere. Vina walked passed him to his room. Still no sign of Phoenix.

"Yo, Phillie, what's up with your girl? She's bugging."

Phillie realized Chase wasn't pretending. "Last night, a friend of mine that works at the 40/40 club said they saw you and Phoenix. She described you even before she saw your picture. I know my girl wasn't fronting. She was sure it was you."

Chase looked at Phillie like she was just as crazy as Vina. "Look, I ain't left this room all night. My word on that! If your friend thought she saw me and Phoenix, she's more than wrong. Ain't no way she saw us together. Cause if she did, she'd be here right now. Vina, you know I would've called and told you I found her."

Vina plopped on the chair next to Chase. "Damn, I just knew I was going to sit and talk to her like old times." Vina's mood changed.

"I'm sorry, Vina. Syncere usually has a photographic memory." Phillie rubbed Vina's head.

"It's not your fault. I've been seeing her everywhere we go, too. Maybe there's a couple walking around New York that look just like Phoenix and his ass."

Chase tried to cheer Vina up. "So what you saying, sis? I ain't cute?" He tickled her and Vina gave in to him. She hadn't seen Chase like this in a long while. Maybe there is hope.

Chases cell phone constantly rang all morning. The only call he answered was Vina's.

"Chase ain't that your phone?"

"It ain't nobody but the 357 crew. So much shit has been happening, I needed a break from them. If it was important, my pager would have went off."

Vina picked up his pager off the table. "Yeah, it would have—if it was on."

Chase jumped up and snatched the pager out her hand. All his head men from all his spots had been burning up his pager since last night. "Damn!" Chase dialed Lynx. "Yow wha'um, my yout'?"

Lynx started talking a mile a minute.

"Whoa! Slow that shit down ... now, what you say?"

"Yo, man, I thought someone offed your ass. I got my men looking all over for you. Where's Cutty? Shit is dry as Desert Storm out this bitch. We ain't had no product since yesterday afternoon. Cutty picked up the earnings and said he'd be back with the stuff, but that niggah never showed up. It's like that at all the spots. We're missing out on dough, man!"

"I know he doesn't like to travel with earnings and product unless shit is low, but not to come back at all? Did y'all call the cells or his pager?"

"When we couldn't reach him by phone or his pager, I sent out the Heavy Hitters to check all his hangouts.

"His girl said she hasn't seen him, either. I hate to say this shit, I know that's your man and shit, but Wayne is the tightest with him; and he tracked Cutty's car parked in the parking lot across the street from the car rental place he uses. That Rajii shit blew my mind cause that lil niggah thought you was the world ... now Cutty's gone with the money and the product."

"This shit ain't happening! It just ain't happening. What the fuck? Mi nevah cyan 'ave peace ... nevah." Lynx figured his boss was about to blow when he heard his accent mid-sentence. "Mi inna de city. Mi soon come ... in a hour or so. Check mi at de west stash house, seen? Mek a call to de Heavy Hitters ... seen ... tell dem meet yuh dere."

"You know Mad Mike is in Australia ... the land down under? And 5-0 swooped up Nigel."

"Yes, mi know ... latah." Chase rose from the table and started ranting and raving in his Jamaican tongue while tugging on his shorts. The veins in his neck protruded outward. His eyes became red and watery.

"Chase, calm down," Vina said. "You look like you're about to bust open. What happened? And talk English."

Chase paced back and forth; couldn't stop tugging on his shorts.

"Nevah inna mi life ... mi done wit dis ... Cha! Ta roti!" He turned to Vina and Phillie. "Mi hafah mek a run." Chase ignored Vina's questions. He went in the room and came out quickly. "Call me if tings turn up." He handed Vina a wad of bills and left.

A SUNKEN SHIP

Rajii sat on the couch consumed by his thoughts. There's got to be a way to turn this shit around in my favor. I already got a body on my hands. Kye wants to take Blizz out, and he's my girl's fucking brother. I still got this bounty shit on my head.

Kye jumped up.

Jamaira tapped Rajii. "Shop, Kye's up."

Kye held his head. "What the fuck?" He caught a rush of dizziness when he stood. His mouth was dry and his head pounded.

"That's what your ass gets for touching my haze. Niggah, you know you ain't ready for that."

"Man, you ain't even got to worry about that no more. Y'all did the shit without me?"

"Yo, Kye, let me holla at you for a minute. This is what I came up with..."

"Yo, you two thought that shit out perfectly."

Jamaira checked her watch. "Shop, it's about that time." Jamaira went downstairs to pull the truck to the back parking lot, just a few feet from Rajii's window. Rajii dropped the comforter out the window.

"Glove up, man."

Kye and Rajii lifted the body and dropped Cutty out the window. They then left the apartment carrying the extra bag that held Cutty's weapons and keys. Once they reached the back of the building, Kye and Rajii lifted Cutty then dropped him in the back of Rajii's truck. They circled the lot. The visitors' lot was just about empty. Rajii searched for cars that didn't look familiar to him. He stepped out and peeked in the cars. Nothing resembled anything that Cutty would drive. They exited the lot and went out the gate. A Pontiac Grand Am was parked at the tip of the driveway. Rajii jumped out and checked to see if the keys fit. Bingo!

"Jamaira, pull over. This is it."

Kye jumped out holding the small bag. "Look, man, I got a plan. You know the back of the East End? There's a dock on the side of that seafood restaurant. I think it's called Dolphin's Cove. The road runs right into the river. We can put this niggah in his own shit and let his ass sink to the bottom. By the time they find his ass, the fish would have eaten his ass up.

"Jamaira doesn't need to be in the car with the body. Drop these guns in the trunk; inside the spare tire. She can drive this and we can drive the truck. We can figure out how we're going to switch the body to this car when we get to the east."

"A'ight. There's a spot I used to take my tricks where the grass is high and that shit looks abandoned. You know that side street off Newfield Avenue, Suggest Lane? The street with those country Bama houses? We can do the switch there."

Rajii popped the trunk of the Grand Am and lifted the floor to drop in the bag of weapons. He recognized the five large Nike Gym Bags right off the back.

Eyes on the Pryze

"Oh, shit! We done hit a goldmine!" He unzipped three bags and showed Kye about three million in cash. He unzipped the other two bags and showed Kye bricks of coke and boulders of crack.

Kye couldn't believe his eyes. "Yo, man, we hood rich!"

Rajii nodded. He didn't tell Jamaira why they needed to go back to the crib. They dropped off the cash and drugs then returned to the vehicles.

"Y'all think this shit we're doing is legal, huh? You two got me sitting in this truck with his ass," Jamaira pointed to the bagged body.

"Come on, let's get this shit done. My nerves are messing with me." Rajii told Jamaira to drive Cutty's car so, if they were stopped, she wouldn't be pinned to the body. "I want you to take the street there. Drive safe, but not paranoid. Park the car on the corner of Newfield and Seaview Avenue and wait. If we don't pull up within ten minutes, bring the car back, go in the house, and call my cell from the house phone. If you don't get an answer, hang up. No messages. Wait for my call." Rajii kissed Jamaira on the forehead. "Be safe and don't worry. Everything's gonna work out."

Rajii took I-95 to Exit 29 then went through the intersection to Seaview Avenue. Jamaira waited; parked where Rajii told her. He flashed his headlights as Kye stuck his hand out the window, signaling Jamaira to follow them. They arrived at Suggest Lane and switched the body from the truck to the car.

"Meet us back on Seaview and Newfield Avenue." Rajii covered the garbage bag with a comforter.

Felisha Bradshaw

Once they reached the dock, Kye noticed the way Rajii looked in the back seat at the lump under the comforter.

"You sure you wanna do this? Cause I can finish the rest."

"Nah, man, we in this till the end."

Kye put the car in neutral. They jumped out and gave the car one good push and sent Cutty out to sea.

"We need to chill for a second and figure out what our next move is going to be."

Rajii agreed.

On the ride back to the crib, they all remained silent. Rajii was thinking about the bounty on his head, and how he was going to get out of it. If there was a way that they could use the money found in Cutty's car to get the bounty off of his head, he surely would comply. He wanted a clean slate with Jamaira, and here he was starting this relationship already keeping secrets from her ... the money.

Jamaira couldn't take her mind off their relationship, either. More precisely, her brother, Blizz, wanting to come between her relationship with Rajii. She knew sooner or later she'd have to face Blizz—and choose one or the other. Having her cake and eating it too would not be an option. *What have I gotten myself in to?*

Kye pondered a way to kill Blizz without it burdening his boy's relationship with his cousin. *Maybe I should put a bounty on that niggah's head!*

None thought twice about the murder they just committed.

BACK TO REALITY

Phillie and Vina combed the city trying to find Phoenix. Every time they got a lead, it went dead. They didn't want to give up, but knew they had to return to Connecticut soon.

"When we find Phoenix and everything's back to normal, there's so much I want to share with you."

"Talk to me, Phillie."

Phillie looked out on the water. "In due time, baby, in due time."

They enjoyed the breeze as they stood on the pier.

***

It didn't take long for Chase to hit home. Lynx, and the other Heavy Hitters, knew Chase wouldn't be in the best of moods. They weren't sure what he expected of them, but they were going to be there for him. Although things sounded a little sheisty, they were willing to stand by him.

Chase stopped at his bank to check his account and safety deposit box—just in case Lynx's theory was true.

I can't believe Cutty would run out with my dough. I was paying him thirty percent of my profits, and whatever he made on his own was his. That's damn near half of what I make. Muthafuckahs ain't never satisfied. Chase opened his safety deposit box and saw that Cutty hadn't been there. Cutty could have taken my money. He had access. Something doesn't add up. Why didn't he take all the money?

Chase headed to the west end spot. He recognized a few cars parked outside the building. When he reached the lobby, the Heavy Hitters waited on the stairs.

"Where's Lynx?"

Dré, one of the Heavy Hitters, stood. "He went to get some cash from his mom's spot. In case you needed it, man. We all have something for you."

The ones he slept most proved the most loyal. Chase nodded. They followed him to the apartment. Demon started barking until the door opened. He rushed Chase, almost knocking him over.

"Hey, boy. I'm here." Demon moved his tray around with his nose. "I know you're hungry." Chase immediately fed his watchdog then opened the windows. He thought he'd left enough food and water, but Chase saw where Demon gnawed through part of the cupboard where his food was kept. When Chase walked to the back room, the furniture was ripped up; dog shit everywhere. "Damn! Call that chick down the hall and see if she wants to work."

Chase opened the closet door. A six-foot safe stood before him. He opened the safe to find it'd been cleared out. He figured the safes at his two other stash houses were more than likely in the same condition.

"Dré, take these keys and feed the dogs at the other spots. Find me a head to clean up the spots."

"A'ight Boss."

Eyes on the Pryze

The two other men stood at attention. They saw sweat forming on Chase's brow. They couldn't wait for Lynx to get there. He was the only person who could calm Chase down. Thankfully, Chase didn't lose it. He calmly pulled up a stool and sat until Lynx arrived.

"Yo, man, let me talk to you." Lynx took Chase into the hallway. "Man, I just found out that your pops is looking for you. He's got some information for you."

"I ain't talk to his doped up ass in years." How would that niggah even know where I'm at? Then he recalled a recent conversation with Cutty.

"Rumor is, he's clean, and your moms...well, your moms passed away," Lynx said.

Chase never looked back when he left New York as a young teen. He hadn't picked up the telephone one time to call his parents. Even though they weren't shit, they were still his parents. Cutty reminded him of that a few weeks ago. He also remembered Cutty talking about how much he missed Jamaica, and that he was getting too old for the game. Even if Cutty kept in contact with his father, Chase wondered what kind of information could his father offer him. Chances were he knew nothing. Chase assumed he was just looking for a handout.

"How did she die? When? Drugs?"

"This was all I found in Cutty's crib." Lynx handed him a piece of paper. "That's how I know. I wanted to tell you when I called, but I didn't think it was the right way to go about it." Lynx left Chase in the hallway with his thoughts.

Chase looked at the paper again, recognizing Cutty's handwriting: Bancroft Pryze (212)-555-1121 ... Have him call before ... A juice stain made the date illegible. Chase read the bottom of the paper ... for a small price he'll do what's right. Chase crumbled up the paper and shoved it in his pocket. What the fuck does that mean ... maybe my father didn't say that ... maybe Cutty was just jotting down something of his own. Whatever the facts may be, at this point it wasn't enough to make Chase call. That shit is in the past ... business is here and now.

"Let's get this shit together. I'll have to call the connect. I don't know what's going to happen with that because he usually only deals with Cutty. I never met him before, so let's see what's what. We'll meet back here in an hour. Page me before you come. I'll put in 911 twice if we get what we need." The Heavy Hitters offered their money to Chase. "Cool, my bredrens, but mi 'ave tings so far. Good looking out. Everything's irie. Lynx, come."

The crew dispersed. Lynx and Chase headed to Cutty's crib.

"I hope I'm not wrong, but I don't just see you as the man that butters my bread, you dig? I hope you don't look at me like it's just business."

"Jus' talk, Lynx. Tings wit us is different. Shoot!"

"If ... if you haven't talked to your father in years, how did Cutty find him or he find Cutty? It's not like Cutty puts his business out there like that. He ain't an easy man to track down."

That's why Chase liked Lynx ... he was a thinker. "Well, I like to keep my business just that ... my business. But I will tell you this; Cutty's been a friend of my father's since they lived in Jamaica as kids. My so-called father got me in some shit with some Colombians I was transporting for, so I had to leave. I met Cutty on the train on my way here.

He put me on. Everything else has me wondering just as much as the next man."

"Did you know Cutty when you were in New York?"

Chase thought about it. "Nah. He knew me by face. They say I look just like my father did when he was a kid. Why all the questions?"

"So, you were on the run for some shit that your father got you in, right?"

Chase shook his head. "I never ran. I left."

Lynx kept going. "...And you just so happen to find his old friend, who never met you before, on the train. He took you in and put you on ... just like that?" Lynx shook his head. "That's too much of a coincidence for me, man. Now that niggah and the second man closest to you are missing and both left with your dough! Think about it, man ... that's all I'm saying."

Chase was young, then; looking for a way out. Cutty gave him a way out. Now Chase questioned it all.

They opened the door to Cutty's apartment. Lynx immediately noticed things were not the way he left them. "Man, somebody's been here. This shit was nice and tidy when I came through."

Chase and Lynx drew their pieces. They searched the rest of the house, but it was empty. Chase locked the door while they went through Cutty's things. During the search, Chase came across the ledger that Cutty used to keep track of the business. Everything appeared in order, but no amount entered for the most recent earnings. This told Chase that Cutty never returned home after the pickup. Chase kept this info to himself. He searched the last page of the book where Cutty kept his connect's number in code.

Cutty used a letter to represent a number, just like a telephone keypad. The code spelled out: Just Put The 51 And Dah 11s in room 515. (578) 512-3117 room 515.

Chase wasn't sure what to tell the connect about Cutty, but knew he had to do something. Chase dialed the number from Cutty's desk phone. "Room 515 please?"

"Who shall I say is calling?"

"Cutty."

The clerk connected him.

"Hola, mi amigo. Que puede yo hacer para usted?"

"Soy amigo de Cutty, y no hablo español."

There was a long pause.

"How did you get this number? Where is Cutty?"

Chase ran down what he thought the man needed to know without telling him his name.

"Cutty set up a plan with me if he ever was to die. The only person I will speak to is the name he gave me. If you are not him, this call will end. What is your name?"

Chase called his voice mail to tape the conversation. "Never mind that. I'll call you again with the name."

The man on the other end yelled out to someone in the background. "Encuentrelo...Deseo hablarle personalmente ...compruebe en esta persona de la persecución." Chase would soon learn what that meant. "Don't dial this number until then." The connect hung up.

"What? What? What did he say about Cutty? Are we in?"

"No."

Lynx left it at that. The 357 were going to experience a long drought. Chase and Lynx headed over to Side Effect lounge to check a few dealers that he sold weight to. Since they only dealt with him, he wanted to see if they had any product they wanted to get off their hands.

Chase called Vina and Phillie and told them that they should continue to look for Phoenix, but they had to check out of the hotel in the next few days and find another living arrangement. Things were getting tight on his end.

THE CLOSER I GET TO YOU

Phoenix and Cahree didn't expect to get so much work in their classes. They had to buckle down and hit the books. Caine spent most of his time with Cahree at the brownstone. Since most of their classes were together, Cahree and Phoenix studied together. Whenever the assignment called for a group effort, they worked together.

"I need a break." Phoenix stared over at Caine sprawled out across her bed.

"Okay, I'll fix us some lunch." Cahree said, glad to get away from the books. She's such a bookworm. What does all this have to do with designing. I no think this is the school for me. I want to sketch ... make clothes ... this no for me.

Phoenix heard Cahree scream. She yelled downstairs. "Cahree, you okay? What's wrong?"

"Nothing." Cahree mumbled her true feelings under her breath. "Nada pero el hecho de que mi padre es un idiota ... puta."

Phoenix and Caine were finally alone. Caine jumped at the opportunity to fill her head with lies. He was sure once he made love to her, she'd be hooked. Then she could serve her purpose, linking him to Chase.

"Caine? Why don't you ever try to make any advances towards me?"

Caine looked in her eyes. "Baby, we cyant start tings if I don't know your past is innah de past. Yuh say mi look like your old mon, but mi know no-ting about 'im, or your feeling for dis mon."

"When I first saw you, I wished you were him. I hoped that he had tracked me down, and was coming to take me back home."

"Why? Yuh run from 'im?"

"Chase and I broke up. I saw him cheating on me with my best friend, Vina. I put off going away to college to be with him, but then that happened. I stopped talking to them both and came to NYU. So, you see, when I saw you I thought you were coming to tell me what I saw wasn't that at all. I can't say that I don't have feelings for him because that would be a lie. But I've moved on. He's a part of my past. I want to have a future with you. I know now that Chase was my childhood love, my young love. It did freak me out that you look so much like him, and that may be the reason I was attracted to you, but you're so different from him. You're so much more mature and you make me feel like a woman. We've done things that I thought I'd experience as a woman. Do you understand? I don't see him in you anymore."

Caine was so happy that Chase fucked up, making it easier to use Phoenix as his pawn. He wanted Chase's empire, and to give the Colombians what they wanted: to watch Chase rise and fall till he had nothing.

"So yuh tink you're ready to start dis wit mi?"

"I'm falling in love with you Caine. I'm ready to be with you."

Caine held her close. "Be mine tonight. Mi love yuh, too. Mi soon come. I want tings to be jus' right." Caine rose from the bed. "Mek we 'ave privacy."

Phoenix walked him to the door. She couldn't wait to share her excitement with Cahree. She swirled Cahree around and began jumping up and down. "Guess what, guess what?"

Cahree joined in. They held hands and swirled in a circle together like schoolgirls on the playground.

"What? What?"

"He finally did it!"

"Did what, P? What did he do?"

"He made the first move. I asked him why he's never tried anything. He was such a gentleman. He said it was because of Chase. When I told him that was the past, he said he loved me and tonight was the night we make things official. I never dreamed I could love anyone but Chase, then I realized I was falling in love with Caine. I didn't go searching for it. It just happened."

Cahree's face froze. Phoenix could tell she wasn't as excited anymore.

"Aren't you happy for me?"

Cahree tried to appear happy for her, but deep down inside she couldn't be. She knew the truth; knew what Caine was up to. "Yes, mami, I am happy. Did joo say to him that joo loved him first?"

Phoenix wondered why she asked. Can't she tell? "Yes! Yes, I told him first. I wanted him to know how I felt. You think I shouldn't have? What's wrong? You say you're happy for me, but you don't look like you are?"

Cahree wanted to blow the whistle on Caine. Instead, she gave Phoenix something to think about.

"Mami, I am just concerned about jor feelings? I know joo wanted him to make the move like joo said, but I never thought joo would want to accept so soon. But joo really made the first move when joo told him joo loved him. Are joo curious that he looks so much like jor old boyfriend? What do joo really know about him? Jes, he is handsome, but what else do joo know?"

Phoenix frowned. Why is she saying this? She looked Cahree in the eye and she saw nothing but concern. Cahree was looking out for her, like a friend should, but she wanted to be with Caine.

"Thanks, Cahree. I know you're worried I may be making the wrong decision. I might even be taking things a little fast but, in my heart, it just seems right. Just like when you meet your Denzel, you will know, too, and then you'll understand." Phoenix smiled at her friend, hoping she would understand. "Cause you know I'm gonna be all up in your business when that shit happens. Ain't nobody gonna mess up my girl's first time. I know you got my back, sweetie, and that's how I know our friendship is gonna always be."

Cahree felt guilty now, but didn't want to take away her friends happiness. She hugged Phoenix, and told her to be careful.

"I'm going to take a long bath, so I can smell real sexy for him. He'll be here in a little while. I'm gonna get ready." Phoenix left to prepare for her night of lovemaking.

A tear fell from Cahree's eye. She flopped on a stool and started talking into the air.

Why daddy? Why use P? All the investigating I did on Chase for you, and it wasn't enough. I got you that Rajii boy. I found out who his trigger man was. I did everything to make you proud; to show you I could be everything you wanted your son to be.

Cahree had gone too far to win over her father. All this for his approval, knowing, with him, a daughter could never replace a son. She should have never approached that girl at Phoenix's old college. Then she would have never known she was leaving to attend NYU.

Cahree wanted to blame everything on everyone else. She blamed Chase for getting her brother shot, which left him in a vegetative state, and for sleeping with Vina. She blamed her father for setting up Phoenix—to get her heart broken. But deep down, she knew she made it all possible. She faked the call about her father wanting to meet her at the café, knowing Caine was looking to "accidentally" let Phoenix see him.

She hadn't planned on growing to genuinely care for Phoenix. Phoenix didn't care that her father was rich and powerful. Cahree finally found a friend who cared about her ... who she was ... someone who accepted her for being Cahree. Finally, she was able to tell someone her dreams. Her father didn't care whether she wanted to be a lawyer, he didn't even care if his daughter became successful; all he wanted was revenge—and didn't care who he used to get it. Cahree wanted to tell Phoenix everything. If she lost her friendship then so be it.

Cahree sat at the counter and cried a while. Then she stood and walked to the bottom of the staircase. The water running in the shower stopped. "Phoenix, when jou're done come talk to me, okay?"

Phoenix stopped at the top of the steps before going to her room. "Okay, be right down."

Pacing back and forth in the living room, Cahree practiced what she'd say; her eyes red from crying. Phoenix came downstairs. She'd put her hair in a beautiful up-do,

Eyes on the Pryze

and wore an elegant black lace one piece with matching garter belt. Seeing how much effort Phoenix put into looking just right for Caine made it harder for Cahree to tell her the truth.

"Come here, mami. I need to talk to joo."

"How do I look?"

Cahree couldn't wait any longer. "P, joo know that I have never had a friend like joo. To be honest, I really never had a friend. And I wanted to tell joo—"

Caine walked in the door. Cahree looked away from him, wondering what he heard.

Caine glared at Cahree. "Mi interrupt someting?"

"It's okay. We can girl-talk later."

Phoenix whispered to Cahree. "We'll talk later. Love you."

Caine looked Phoenix up and down. "Yuh look beautiful," he said then scooped her up like a princess.

If Cahree hadn't known the truth about Caine, she would have wished she was being swept away. But she knew better. Caine was no prince.

Cahree had to get out of that house. Had to. Shopping always made her feel better. She loved the vintage Village stores. She passed a few sex toy stores, but felt too embarrassed to go in—until she ran into a flamboyant store clerk smoking a cigarette outside.

"Go on in, girlfriend! They ain't gonna bite you. Unless you want them to."

"I know but..."

The clerk flicked his cigarette and took her under the arm and escorted her into he store. She hesitated at first but, when she noticed it was almost empty, she gave in to her curiosity.

"Now, what you looking for? Replacing that man?"

"Nooo, I don't have one."

The clerk said, "Me either, but I'm looking."

Cahree was tickled by his admission. He took her to the back wall. Cahree's face turned beet red looking at the various sizes of dicks on the wall ... in bins ... some were out of the box and on display.

"Here, feel this one," the clerk handed her a nine inch dildo with prongs. "It feels like the real thing, doesn't it?" Cahree whispered in his ear. He jumped back. "Oh, baby girl, you don't need all that! Let's get you a starter kit ... something small."

The clerk threw in some cleaner and complimentary lubricants then discreetly brown bagged everything. Cahree found a temporary replacement for her dream man, and called it Denzel.

RAJII

After that night, the bond among Rajii, Jamaira, and Kye was unbreakable. Although her mother didn't approve, Jamaira moved in with Rajii. They had been intimate but not completely. Foreplay was the only thing on the menu once Jamaira saw what he was working with. Inside the house, they started calling Shop by his real name.

"Regardless to what Blizz says or does, he has violated. I don't want to hear that shit," Kye said.

Rajii had grown frustrated with Kye and the whole situation. "Jamaira's moms keeps hitting her up on the cell to make good with him. I think Jamaira wants to, but doesn't, and it's because of us. I don't know what to tell her. I love my girl. I see she's hurting."

Kye saw it, too. But it was what it was. He didn't want things like this. Blizz made them this way ... not him. And Kye refused to go back on his word to Shotz.

"On the real, she should make amends with her brother." Kye's empathy shocked Rajii. "Especially since he won't be around much longer."

Rajii shot Kye a quick look. He knew it was hopeless. Blizz was a dead man. Rajii changed the subject.

"What are we going to do with all this dough? I know your ass needs a new ride, and you can hit off Shotz's people, too."

"Yeah, man. That's what's up. But how we gonna grind with that bounty on your head? We can't bag all them niggahs."

"We got enough to feed all them niggahs." Kye looked at Rajii like he was crazy. "Nah, just listen. We got a cool three million in cash even after we hit off your peeps and get you and Jamaira a nice whip. Then we got about another two mill or so in bricks, right?"

"And?"

"Just watch me work!" Rajii kept Cutty's phone in case he needed it. "Hold up." He went to his room to get it. Jamaira was sound asleep, which was good. She didn't need to know what was about to go down.

Rajii waved Cutty's phone when he sat next to Kye again.

"Man! Why'd you keep that? I thought we sunk that shit."

"I knew I'd need this. Yo, the shit I'm about to put in play is waterproof. Too bad that rental wasn't." Rajii's smile scared even Kye. He searched the phone for Chase's number. Rajii knew only Cutty had this number. "See?" Rajii showed Kye.

"What you gonna do with that?"

Rajii dialed the number. "Yo, Chase, I ... I ... gotta warn you about Cutty."

Chase knew the number but didn't recognize the voice. "Who the fuck is this? Where's Cutty?"

Rajii started whispering between gasps. "It's me ... Rajii ... Cutty got me in this fucking warehouse. Yo, that niggah is crazy. I don't have time ... just watch your back, Chase. He said he's gonna kill you."

Eyes on the Pryze

"What? Kill me? Got you where?"

Rajii hurried his last words out. "I'll call you back. Stay by the phone. I gotta go. He's coming." Rajii hung up then turned off the phone.

Kye sat with his mouth wide open. He couldn't believe Rajii just called Chase; more amazed by what he told him.

"Yo! What you do that for?" Rajii finally shared his plan with Kye. "That shit just might work!"

FAMILY CAN BE YOUR WORST ENEMY

"I will, Ma. I already called her four times today, four times yesterday and the day before that and the day before that. If she wants to talk to me, she'll call back." Blizz grew tired of his mother pressuring him to make amends with his younger sister. His mother didn't know all the things Jamaira said to him. *I got feelings, too.* An incoming call on his cell interrupted Blizz's thoughts. "Ma, I'll see you later. You need something?"

Strangely, his mother, who had never accepted money from him, asked her son to cover her bills this month. Blizz hesitated then agreed then answered his incoming call.

"Yo! Tings dry inna de Side Effect. M.D. called and 'im say a client called 'im for some candy. 'im say 'e give 'er a lick and dem gals come fi it after."

"No candy at Side Effect? Something ain't right. Tell M.D. to call me."

Caine got on his case about setting shit right with Rajii. "Yo, yuh bettah mek tings right. Time is tickin."

Blizz knew if he didn't work fast, he'd have more than Rajii and Kye to worry about. *One more time then I give up. I'll just have to find another way.* Blizz sat in his car and dialed Jamaira.

"Hello...you've reached Jamaira. Sorry I'm not available to answer your call. But if you leave a quick message and number, if I choose to, I will return your call. If I don't return your call then it's obvious."

"Whatever. I'm trying to holla at you, Jam. I said I was sorry. What else can I say?" Blizz hung the phone up and tossed it on the passenger's seat. Just as he was about to pull off, his cell rang again. Yeah, I thought so. "Holla at cha boy!"

It wasn't Jamaira.

"What's up, B?" M.D. went on to confirm the serious drought at Side Effect. "Rumor has it that niggah, Chase, got beat for a few million. His boy cut out on him with his product and his dough. They say he ain't got no connect cause the dude that bounced with his shit was the only person who made the transactions with them Colombians he cops from. Yo, when I served that chick, they all came running at me. I made loot just sitting in my ride. Caine said to check you. What you need?"

Blizz smiled widely. He had a plan to shift Caine's mind off of Rajii and Kye.

"M.D., I got something I need you to do—and don't fuck up. If you do, shit won't sit easy with me or Caine, and I don't think you want that."

M.D. didn't fear Blizz much but, when he heard Caine's name, he listened.

"Nah, man. Whatever you need."

After Blizz told M.D. his plan, M.D. wished he'd never made the call.

BACK TO THE LAB

Chase sat back and tried to swallow what Rajii fed him. Did he say Cutty wanted to kill me? What warehouse? What the fuck is going on? Chase tried to call Cutty's phone, but it went straight to voice mail. Why did he turn the phone off?

The bar was desolate. Side Effect usually held a decent sized crowd, equal to Novella's, every night. Coke was on the main menu. The crowd generally consisted of old timers; either there to shoot the shit and get drunk or trick up whatever money they had left. The dealers in the bar made sure there was enough candy for them to buy for the women. Today was different. Normally, Chase would walk up in the spot and dealers would nod at him to let him know they were straight. Today, he didn't recognize the tall, slim brother serving candy.

Chase and Lynx sat at the far end of the bar. Chase called over one of the regular bartenders.

"Yow, Venus!"

Venus stopped cleaning the glasses and approached Chase. "What's up, Chase? You know you owe me for a few nights work. Tips in this bitch have been scarce. Can't keep nobody in here except for these hos." She pointed to the tricks at the other end of the counter hanging around the seated unfamiliar face.

Eyes on the Pryze

"Shit's real tight now. I came to check and see who had what."

"They've been chilling. But this niggah over here has been keeping some of the business around for a few days."

Chase eyed him up and down. He gave Venus some ends to make up for her loses, and for the information. "Lynx, give her your cell number so she can holla at us."

Venus smiled at Chase. Satisfied with her pay, she added, "They call him M.D., and good looking."

Chase tapped Lynx on the side of his leg and nodded. They slowly approached M.D.

"Yo, partner!"

M.D. ignored Lynx.

"Yow! Wha'um my yout? Ya nah 'ear my bwoy?"

M.D. knew this was the man Blizz told him to look out for.

"My bad. What's good, dread? What you need?"

With a shoo of his hand, Chase ordered the women to leave. Chase stood in front of the man with Lynx tight on M.D.'s back.

"Yuh see dis?" Chase referred to the establishment. "Tings nah run in 'ere wit out my tings, seen?"

M.D. looked around for a way out; just in case the dread and his goon got it twisted.

"Dem my tings?"

Lynx dug his hands into the man's coat pocket, looking for the 357 stamp on the baggies.

"Nah, man, this ain't your shit." M.D. shifted in his seat, trying not to display his fear.

"If dis nah mines, what mek yuh tink yuh cyan sell in 'ere?"

"I only came to serve one of my girls outside, but then I got rushed so I just chilled here?"

"Mi outta luck. Someone teef my product, but yuh still cyan gwan like we fam, seen? If yuh no work fi mi den yuh no work dis place."

Lynx put the man's drugs into his inside coat pocket.

"Yo, man, that's my shit."

"What the fuck you say? Niggah, you ain't listening. This ain't the place for you. This here spot is ours so that shit is ours, feel me?" Lynx revealed the piece on his hip. M.D. backed off. "So unless you here to look out for our interests, you gets none of these." Lynx tapped his coat pocket.

Chase and Lynx started to walk away.

"I can get you something till your shit comes in, depending on the amount."

Chase looked at Lynx, unsure if he could trust this buster.

"So you got it like that, huh? We don't bag garbage." Lynx was way ahead of Chase.

"Good, cause I don't sell garbage."

Chase called one of the girls over who he knew his man dealt to, asking her if this shit was as good as his. She nodded. Lynx took out his cell and M.D. gave him his number.

"What kind of weight you talking, so I know what I have to work with?"

"Ten bricks," Chase said, testing him.

"That's all? Ten bricks won't hold you for long." M.D. looked around the bar. The crowd had grown larger.

Chase looked at Lynx.

"We'll judge that," Lynx said. "Ten bricks now and, if the shit is right, we'll be back. What's your price, and don't take us for no suckers."

"Fourteen a brick."

"We'll give you a call in about two hours." Chase and Lynx left the bar to check out this M.D. character.

"So, what cha think?" Chase contemplated the buy. With everything that was going down, he knew he had little choice.

"You want me to check out other options before we fuck with this dude?"

Fuck it. It's only temporary. "I know M.D. ain't the man behind the scene. He's probably gonna skim off the top to make some PC and it might put him in a better price range. So, I don't think he'll fuck us. Let's hit him up once we get to the crib."

Chase's invitation surprised Lynx. He had never been to the spot Chase called home. When they pulled up to Chase's home, Lynx turned to Chase.

"You live here?" It wasn't what Lynx expected. The units were all in a community. The grounds were old and vines grew up the sides of the buildings.

"Yo, I'm a humble niggah. Y'all waste y'all money on living like rich men."

Lynx laughed. "You need to un-humble yourself, then. No wonder you never let niggahs see where you live."

"This is a castle compared to..." Chase put his key in the door and they stepped in. Lynx's mouth dropped again.

Felisha Bradshaw

He walked out to the patio then stepped in again, feeling like a kid in a candy store. Chase's living room was laid out. His system took up one whole wall; the speakers were club-size. His four six-foot CD/DVD racks took up another wall. The first two held all reggae music from some group named Alpha and Omega Sound System to Ziggy Marley and the Melody Makers. The other rack was filled with Hip-Hop and R&B from Aaliyah to Young Wun. The DVD racks hyped Lynx most. Chase had one rack filled with every movie you could think of.

"Nah, man, tell me you ain't on that shit! I could sit here and watch these all day!" Lynx sifted through the fourth rack. Every so often he'd scream, "Oh, shit! Where'd you find this one?" Lynx couldn't believe the entire fourth rack was filled with Karate flicks. "Yo, 18 Bronzemen! That was the shit." Lynx continued looking around the living room taking in Chase's original African American oil paintings and African carvings. Chase's sectional couch with fill-in ottomans rounded out the rest of the room. There had to be at least thirty-five pieces to the sectional. "Damn, niggah, you act like you be having company like a muthafuckah."

On the far corner of the wall was a fifty-inch plasma TV on a swivel base with a surround sound system. "That's what's Up?" Lynx then stepped in the kitchen. Chase had an island counter unit put in the middle of the kitchen floor. All the appliances were stainless steel. The refrigerator was double-door with a TV in it. "What! This shit should be on MTV Cribs. For sure!" Chase laughed at Lynx and followed behind him, getting a kick out of watching Lynx's reactions. Lynx walked the long hallway to the back bedroom. Chase turned the guest room into an office. The walls had pictures of him and Phoenix, and one poster size picture of the 357 Crew. Chase's bedroom looked like something out of a magazine. "Yo! This is the shit!" Chase laughed at him. Chase finally was able to get a word in edgewise.

"Oh, now it's the shit! That's what's wrong with y'all niggahs. You want everybody to know what y'all got. See me, my shit is regular on the outside, but I put my money on the inside. I do shit for me, not other muthafuckahs."

Lynx understood what he meant. Flossing was for suckers. Chase and Lynx headed back to the living room.

"It's about that time. What we gonna do? We gonna check this niggah or what?"

Chase thought about everything on the way to his crib: the Rajii shit, Cutty missing and the rumors circulating about him, the message from his pops, and Phoenix. His empire began to crumble. He knew what he had to do.

"Call that niggah and give him the go-ahead."

GIRLFRIENDS

Caine loved the layout in the guest room. The sweet scent of mango kiwi candles burned in every corner.

Phoenix wanted to please him in every way possible. She drew him a bath then undressed him. After sensuously bathing Caine, she dried him off and oiled his body. She loved the way he glistened in candlelight.

Caine hadn't realized how beautiful she was until now. The curves of her body made him stiff. He tried to flip her on to the bed.

"No. This night isn't about me. It's about me loving you."

Phoenix turned on her slow CD; slid over to him until she was at the end of the bed. Phoenix signaled him to sit up. He followed her lead. She stood in front of him and began her erotic dance, slowly slipping off her lingerie until she was bare. She stood in front of him and turned around. Phoenix bent over to touch her toes. Phoenix prayed she wasn't making a fool of herself or giving him the wrong impression. Caine loved every moment of her show. He couldn't believe some of the things Phoenix could do with her legs.

"Damn, baby!"

This encouraged Phoenix to give him a lap dance. Caine couldn't take her gliding back and forth and gyrating on his lap. He laid back and pulled her on top of him, but

Phoenix had other plans. She stood over him and started rubbing her breasts, moaning and groaning. She then moved on to her midsection. She masturbated for Caine until she reached a climax. Her knees buckled and she lay beside him.

He looked so delicious to her. She began rubbing and sucking his nipples. She moved her tongue down his midsection to his abs and landed her tongue in his belly button. Caine's body quivered under her. He prayed she'd move farther down. Yes!

Phoenix had been practicing for weeks for this moment. She held the end of his shaft and squeezed. She took the tip of him into her mouth then nibbled and sucked until Caine couldn't take it. He guided her head to take more of him in. She obliged. She cuffed his balls and massaged them as her mouth slowly glided up and down. As his groans increased, so did her speed.

Caine held on to her hips and exploded inside her. Not once did she think to use a condom. She gyrated until she came a second time. Caine then flipped her on her stomach. She threw her legs up until they met the headboard. Caine wanted to bang her brains out, but knew he had to win her heart. He made love to her. Phoenix came so many times she started crying.

"I love you. Caine, I love you." She held him in her arms until the candles in the room melted down to nothing.

Phoenix stared at her man as he slept. Never before had she experienced multiple orgasms. She lost count after the fourth one. Phoenix lay in his arms and dreamed of every tomorrow with her new man.

In the other bedroom, Cahree was working Denzel. At first, she winced in pain. But after using the lubricant, it felt good. She never knew she could please herself like that.

THE DROP

Chase and Lynx met M.D. at the bar.

"The shit is in the rental space; on the back seat in a duffel."

Chase sent Lynx to check the product, and a bar chick to sample it. Lynx returned and gave Chase the go-ahead. They were back in business.

After hitting off the 357 Crew, Chase called it a day. He was glad that one of his burdens was off his back, but his mind was still heavy. Phoenix hadn't been found yet.

"Where are you, baby?" Even with the stuff going on in his life right now, he thought and prayed for her only. I need you in my life right now. Chase knew only she could ease his mind. She had to know that he worshiped the ground she walked on. But all he heard over and over again in his head was: it's over! Chase refocused.

He hadn't heard anything on the streets about M.D. That made him nervous. A niggah that could come up with ten bricks in less than two hours, and good shit at that, should be known. I gotta find out who he's running with. Chase made a few calls to a few big boys, but came up with nothing. Maybe he's from outta town? He knew if that was the case, it would be damn near impossible to find out his M.O.

Lynx hadn't checked in to update Chase with the sales. He wanted to trust Lynx, but look where trust had taken him. His two closest boys fucked him royally. Thinking of them made him call Cutty's cell phone again. That muthafuckah ain't turn that shit on yet? Chase hung up the phone. He decided not to leave a message; no telling who would get it. He placed another call to check in with Phillie and Vina, praying they had good news.

"Hey, V. Where y'all at?"

Vina was mellow, but Chase heard chaos and laughter in the background. "What's up, Chase? We're still in the Village. We're staying with Phillie's friend, Lex … and Genisis. That's Lex's roommate. But Genisis is a medical student, so she's hardly here. She's cool, though."

"Any news?"

"Well, Lex found out that Phoenix is here. Her boy, Chris, put it out there that we were looking for Phoenix. But she's not to be approached, just watched." Vina's mood changed. "A girl that lives in her dorm says that she's been hanging tough with this Puerto Rican chick named Carmen, and that she was a rich girl. They say they are on some money kick. But that's all we got so far? I know Phoenix wanted to be a designer when we talked about opening a boutique, but NYU wasn't the place for that. What could she be taking that would send her in that direction?"

Chase felt bad because when Phoenix told him about her dream of owning a boutique, the first thing he thought was to buy one for her. He never asked what she was doing to get there on her own. He knew this was one of the areas where he needed to step up his game. He needed to realize that she had dreams of her own, and everything wasn't for sale.

Eyes on the Pryze

"I never listened to what she said about her dreams. I just focused on making them come true. That's fucked up, huh?"

"Chase, ain't nothing wrong with that. Don't worry. I'm gonna go down to the registrar's office and what they call an academic advisor. They'll tell me what I would need to take to make Phoenix's dream come true her way. Then we can narrow down the classes she would need to take; making it easier for us to find her. Just sit tight and let baby sis do her thing." Chase was silent. "Chase, you know she loves you. Everything is gonna workout for the best. You'll see."

"A'ight. Keep me posted. If you need me, call me, okay? One."

Chase lay back and thought more about Phoenix. His thoughts were interrupted by an incoming call.

"Yo, Chase!" Rajii's voice was raspy and somewhat unclear. He talked so low, it was hard to make out what he said. "I gotta make this quick. He found out his phone was missing. It won't be long before he figures out I have it." Rajii coughed into the phone. "I think Cutty killed Mad Mike. I knew that niggah went crazy. He just came in with Mike's chain on his neck. I know Mike ain't part with his shit. When he came in here, he had mad duffels. He took the earning from me that night he had me meet him on the north at the gas station. I dropped my car in the lot and rode with him. He said you wanted it that way because my car was hot. When we first got here, he told me I had to put some shit over my eyes cause this spot was a place only you and him know about. It's some kind of ... wait ... I hear something."

The phone went dead.

"Rajii! Rajii!" Chase slammed the phone shut, hoping that Rajii was alright. I knew my man wouldn't run out on me. Everything Lynx said about Cutty ran through his mind. But why? He took me in and, in return, I took that niggah outta some shit. We've been through mad bullshit together. We built this empire and... Just then, he thought about their last call. He was harsh on him. He knew Cutty was a grown ass man—his main man—but he'd spoken to him like he was his stoolie. But damn, he knows how I get when shit gets hectic ... Cha!

"Yo, man, why you ain't tell me that shit before?" Lynx was pissed at Chase. Shit just didn't settle with him.

"We was doing so much shit, I forgot. Then the bar shit went down with this M.D. cat. But when I got this call, I knew that I had to call you; before something else went down to prolong me telling you. So, I'm telling you now! Watch your back. Tell 357 to do the same; while I figure this shit out."

Lynx worried that Chase wasn't telling him everything.

"What place is young Raj talking about?"

"I don't know."

BLIZZ MAKES AMENDS

Blizz set his plan in motion to get Jamaira to talk to him. He just missed Jamaira late one night when she came home to pick up a few things. She was his only link to Rajii and Kye. Things were just too quiet on their end. Blizz didn't have a clue where Rajii lived, and Kye hadn't been to his apartment in a long while. He knew they had to be together.

"Hey, sis. I finally caught you, huh?"

Jamaira huffed into the phone. "What do you want, Blizz?"

"I know you got my messages. I figured I'd give you time to think about what I said."

"Look, Blizz, I ain't doing this for you. I couldn't care less if I never talked to you. I'm doing this on the strength of Mommy. She asked me and I promised I would. So say what you got to say."

"Baby sis, I know I've been hard on you. I don't want to control your life, I just want you to have one. Sometimes I forget that you're not a baby anymore. But in my eyes, that's all I see ... my baby sis. I want the best for you. It's so hard separating my street life from my home life. I've done so much; seen so much. I thought I was protecting you from it all." Blizz took a deep breath. "I love you, sis. I really love you. That's all I wanted to say. That, and I need you in my life. I need you to forgive me."

"I'm not the only one that you need to apologize to. You hurt Kye so much. He's family. We grew up with him. Y'all used to be so close. You forgot that bid you did? He carried you. He never forgot you when he was hustling. He kept money on your books. Bought your feet, kept you up on what was happening on the streets, and he was the only person out of your boys that even visited you. And you shitted on him! You killed his best friend, Blizz. And for what? Recognition from that silent partner of yours? So what you did a bid with him. Kye did a bid on the outside with you!

"I don't know if I can forgive you just like that. I love you, too. Yeah, you were hard on me ... too hard, but you're my only brother. I still love you. Right now that's all I can say. You know I love Rajii and you have to respect that, too. I'm going to be with him whether you like it or not. So if you can't handle that then ain't no use in making amends."

Blizz tried to get his words out. Not because he was feeling emotional, but because he hated what he had to say. "I, I understand. I know I have to make things right with Kye and Rajii. They are major players in your life, and if you say you love Rajii then I have to accept it. I don't have to like it, but I will accept it. I want you to be a part of my life."

Jamaira was happy to hear Blizz coming to his senses, but she didn't know if he truly meant it. Blizz and Jamaira talked a few more minutes then hung up.

Now how the hell am I gonna tell Rajii and Kye that I spoke to Blizz? They made a vow to each other that secrets would only destroy their bond, so she had to come clean. Jamaira got out of bed and went to do what was right. "What y'all looking all sneaky about?"

Eyes on the Pryze

Kye looked over at Rajii.

Rajii smiled. "We're just bugging. We're prank calling."

She sat between her two favorite people. "Raj, I got something I want to tell you." Rajii sat up. "I talked to Blizz a few seconds ago."

This triggered Kye. "What the fuck you do that for?"

"Yo, man, watch your mouth. You better fall back!"

Kye's reaction didn't surprise Jamaira. She knew how he felt.

"I had to calm my mother's nerves, Kye. I promised her I would accept his next call."

"Sorry, Jam. It's just when I hear his name, it gets me all solid inside. Go ahead, cuz, talk to my man ... I'ma make me a sandwich." Kye headed to the kitchen.

Jamaira told Rajii everything. When Kye overheard what she said, a tear fell from his eye. It felt good hearing Jamaira had his best interest at heart. Kye loved his cousin dearly, but nothing Blizz said could bring back Shotz. Fuck that! There's gonna be slow singing and flower bringing. Kye finished making his sandwich as he sang the rest of Biggie Smalls' rap.

Rajii empathized with Jamaira over the wedge he caused between her and Blizz. After all, Blizz was her brother; her only brother.

"Ma, I knew for a while that you held off talking to your brother cause of us. You don't have to apologize for talking to him. As far as Kye ... he'll get over it. He's hurting, but he has mad love for you." Rajii hugged Jamaira.

THE CLOSER I GET TO YOU: Part Two

Phoenix and Cahree were walking the campus grounds when Lex ran into them.

"Hola, mami? Can I get in where I fit in?" Cahree was not insulted by Lex's advances, but let her know she didn't swing like that.

"Sorry, mami, ain't nothing over here jor size. But thanks for the compliment."

Lex was intrigued by her smile and forwardness. "Oh, did I give you a compliment? So, you saying me hollering at you is a compliment ... am I that fly?"

Her quick wit caught Cahree off guard. "Nah, I just wanted joo to know that I took it as a compliment that, as a woman, joo find me attractive."

Lex tried to keep the conversation going while Chris took out his camera phone. "You both are beautiful. Can I get a picture of y'all with me?" She looked directly at Cahree. "I want to dream of what you won't give me." Cahree looked at Phoenix. They struck a pose and Lex jumped in between them. "So, where y'all heading?" Phoenix told her that they were between classes, and were going to lunch. "We haven't seen you guys at the dorm, cause I would've remembered those pretty faces." Lex laid it on thick. She knew that was the best way to keep the conversation going with women.

Eyes on the Pryze

"Oh, we live in the West Village; around Bleecker Street."

"What are you guys studying?"

Cahree wasn't enthused to talk about her major since she considered dropping out and going to a fashion and design school. But Phoenix loved talking about her dream.

"Business. I want to own my own boutique. Cahree here is having a major problem with deciding what her major will be. I think she wants to do more of the clothes designing thang. So, you both go to NYU?"

Lex admitted she was procrastinating; going part-time the last few semesters. Chris loved the thought of designing clothes more than running the business. But his major was law. They shared a few more words and said their goodbyes.

"See you around."

Cahree and Phoenix waved goodbye.

Lex immediately called home to update Phillie on the progress they made. "Hey, Vina, I saw your missing person. She's cool peeps. I know what her degree is in and I have the street she lives on. I'm about to head over to the Student Life Center at NYU to find out the core requirements for her degree. She's taking Business."

"Aw! I knew I should've went with you guys. Doesn't that narrow things down a bit?"

Lex explained it made things a lot easier because the Business Department had its own area and buildings. "Get atcha soon."

MO' MONEY, MO' MONEY

Chase's pager buzzed like crazy.

"Yo, hit me up! We gotta get this candy before the kids leave."

"What's good?"

Lynx was excited about product moving so fast. The dry period made the baseheads come out like roaches. "Yo, we need to check M.D. again. Shit's pumping like oil wells out this bitch."

Chase urged Lynx to meet him at his crib. He wanted more product, but hesitated to kick the amount he needed to spend to a niggah he didn't know. His mind worked overtime. He tried not to care about the balled up piece of paper still in his pants pocket. *After all this time, he wanna check for me? At least things are changing for the better. Gonna see Phoenix soon, and my product is moving.* Chase took a deep breath and started to relax until he heard a horn outside his window. He signaled to Lynx then went down to meet him.

"What you think about this cat? Can you trust him with all that dough?"

Chase shrugged. "That shit's been on my mind all day. He did come through when he could have bounced, but we ain't talking ten bricks. That shit didn't last. I need to supply all my spots. Everybody's gotta eat and gotta get paid."

Eyes on the Pryze

"I went through all the connects I could think of. Either the price was too high or they wanted to hit us with some shit that would take us weeks to distribute. I know you don't like to sit on too much product. So I guess M.D. is the cheapest and safest way to go. The question is, can we trust him?"

"But this buster got shit, and it's a hundred percent. It's up to you. I don't want to tell you what to do with your shit. I don't need that kind of guilt on my chest if shit don't go right. I hate the way that shit sounds, but you know I gotta keep it real with you."

Chase understood. He knew this was his game and the way he played it would fall on him and only him. "Let's just see what this cat says, so we can make moves. Let's hope it's on the up and up. Call him."

Lynx nodded and dialed M.D.

Chase went ahead with the buy. He spent well over two million with this cat. Desperate situations called for desperate measures. He made sure that Lynx rode with him to make the buy. M.D. hadn't planned on that, so he stopped at a gas station to sneak a call to Blizz.

"Yo, man, this cat got his boy riding with me to make the buy. What you wanna do?"

Blizz knew he couldn't send a little boy to do big boy things. "Man, you know your ass can fuck shit up! I'ma call you back in about two minutes. Tell me what he wants and I'ma tell you that, with a purchase that large, he has to wait a day. Drop that bitch off and come check me. I'ma give you twenty bricks to bring back to them so it shows good business. You dig?"

M.D. followed his instructions. Lynx wasn't too happy until M.D. told him he'd give him bonus bricks till the real shipment came in.

"Good looking, son!"

M.D. dropped Lynx back at the bar. Lynx called Chase and broke down the deal to Chase and their appointment tomorrow. Chase started to mellow out.

"Maybe this cat is on the up and up."

The way M.D. conducted business reminded Chase of how Colombians did business. He was more curious than ever to know who was M.D.'s connect. That kind of weight can only come from one type of dealer. Colombians. Chase shook off the thought, and lay back thinking of Phoenix.

FACE-TO-FACE

Lex did some investigating and narrowed down Phoenix's classes. Two classes were main core requirements, one right after the other, and the classrooms were side-by-side. Lex and Chris staked out the place while they waited for Vina and Phillie. Vina was so anxious, she started dancing in place. She couldn't wait to finally tell Phoenix the truth.

Cahree and Phoenix had plans to meet Caine in the Village for lunch. Phoenix had been looking at the clock on the wall for the last twenty minutes. Phoenix leaned over to Cahree.

"Ugh! When is this man gonna shut up?"

Cahree tried to muffle her giggle. "I know blah, blah, blah. That's all I hear." Cahree didn't care what reason Phoenix had for wanting to leave, even if the reason was Caine. She was ready to go when they got there. The only thing keeping her at NYU was Phoenix. They gathered their books and headed out the door.

"Finally!"

Vina saw the door open and stared in every face. Each one that passed made her stomach flutter. Cahree headed out the door with Phoenix in tow. Phoenix and Cahree were so engaged in conversation, Phoenix didn't even see Vina. Vina tapped her on the shoulder with tears in her eyes. Phoenix turned in her direction and dropped her books.

Vina tried to hug her. Phoenix smacked her. "How dare you. You bitch!"

Vina held the side of her face. "Phoenix. Please. I can explain. I know what you think, but you're wrong!"

"Wrong! You fucked Chase. I saw him carry you into the house. I called him after he left your house. He lied. He said he was on the other side of town, and I'm wrong? Bitch, please."

"Something happened the night before. I need to tell you, then you'll understand."

Phoenix stepped to Vina; she now cried, too. "I thought we were sisters. I thought we were more than that. You want me to understand? I don't give a fuck what you have to say! Happened ... I know what happened." Cahree stepped in and tried to calm Phoenix down. "Nah, Cahree, she deserves to get the business!"

"P, calm down. People are starting to gather. Just talk to her in private."

Phoenix picked up her books. "Talk to her. You know what I told you, Cahree. Talk to her. If that bitch comes near me again, I'll talk to her alright. You coming Cahree? Cause I'm out!"

Cahree handed Lex a piece of paper then walked off.

Vina fell against the wall and slid to the ground. She couldn't say another word.

Phoenix looked back. "Drama queen!"

Phillie picked up Vina and held her close. "What the fuck are y'all looking at!" She shielded Vina from the crowd.

Lex just stood there with the paper in her hand. Although she'd only known V for a little while, she felt bad for her.

Eyes on the Pryze

Chris was loving the chaos. It was right up his alley, but he, too, felt sorry for Vina. "Come on, ma. Tomorrow's another day."

Phillie agreed. "We can let her think about what you said and try again tomorrow."

Vina shook her head. "No! I want to go home. Phillie, let's just go home."

Chris wanted to know what was on the paper. Lex opened it, and they read it.

Give this to Vina. 1141 Bleecker Street.

She handed the paper to Vina. "Don't give up now. You came all this way to get your friend back. Stick to it or you'll regret it."

Through watery eyes, Vina read the paper. She hated Cahree being Phoenix's shoulder to cry on and new best friend, but she appreciated what she did for her.

"See, baby, things will work out. You'll see," Phillie said.

"We have to call Chase."

They returned to Lex's place.

"Chase, we saw Phoenix. ... No, I talked to her. I tried to, at least. She wouldn't talk to me. ... No, she was with that Puerto Rican girl. She hit me. ... No, with her hand; slapped me across my face. She wouldn't listen to me. ... I couldn't tell her that. Too many people around. I tried."

Chase asked a million questions, and caused Vina to relive the incident and cry again. Phillie took the phone and gave Chase the address.

"I think you both need to be there. It's gonna take both of you to wear her down."

Chase told Phillie he'd be there first thing in the morning.

THE GREAT ESCAPE

Rajii and Kye sat on the edge of Rajii's bed playing Madden 2006 while Jamaira cooked dinner. Having to stay in the house was getting the best of them.

"I think it's been long enough. Make the call."

Rajii agreed. He loved his girl, but he needed some time to himself. Rajii needed a haircut, and his hands were just itching to go shopping. Rajii went into character.

"Yo, Chase!" This time he didn't whisper.

"Rajii, that you?" Chase wondered where Cutty was since Rajii was coming in loud and clear.

"I made it out. I called my boy, Kye, and he's on his way to pick me up? I was able to grab three duffel bags—couldn't get them all. Sorry, man. I should've known better."

"It's a'ight, man. You okay? Where you at?"

"He took me to the city; to a warehouse in the Meat District, but I made it to 125th. I'ma take a few dollars to get a haircut and shit. I look straight-up gutter. At least the swelling is going down. I wish I could take a bath."

"Check into Hotel Chelsea. They might ask for ID, so get someone to get the room for you. I'll be in the city by morning. They found Phoenix."

"Found her?"

"I'll fill you in when I get there. Glad you a'ight, man. One!"

"So, what happened man? Why you say New York?" Kye asked. Rajii sat deep in thought, feeling uneasy. "Yo! What happened?"

Rajii stood. "We gotta get to the city. He told me to check in Hotel Chelsea, and he'll see me in the morning. Jamaira will have to stay in another room, so things don't look suspicious."

Kye was glad to be getting out of the house. Jamaira did a good job at keeping up his braids, but he could use a shape up.

"Ma, stop what you're doing. We got a run to make."

"But, Rajii, we're supposed to meet Blizz for drinks after dinner."

That slipped Rajii's mind. But it worked out perfectly. "Call him and tell him we're going to New York, and we'll have drinks there. Make sure he packs an overnight bag, and be ready in an hour."

Rajii filled Kye in on his plan. A devilish grin consumed Kye's entire face.

"Stop it, man, you look like the Joker."

LIVING JUST ENOUGH...FOR THE CITY

Phoenix walked to her car in fury.

"That bitch must be crazy! How she even know where to find me? I know my mother didn't tell her ... if she knows ... Ugh!"

Cahree walked behind her without saying a word.

"I should've scratched her eyes out! She has something she wants to tell me, then I'll understand? What? That bitch is a done deal!"

Phoenix got in the car and slammed the door. Cahree jumped in the passenger's side. Phoenix forgot Cahree was with her. Phoenix raced in and out of traffic like a New York cab driver. Cahree hated buckling up, because it wrinkled her clothes, but today was different.

"What the fuck was she doing with Phillie. Since when? You know, Cahree, she better be glad I bounced because I was about to really let loose on her ass." Phoenix looked over at Cahree. "Girl, are you listening to me?"

"Yeah, P, I hear joo and he hears joo and she hears joo. We all hear joo." Cahree pointed to the other drivers at the stoplight.

P looked over at the car beside her and laughed. "Yeah, I am loud, huh?"

"So, I guess we aren't going to class, huh?"

Phoenix was so mad, she forgot they had another class.

Eyes on the Pryze

"I just wanted to get away from her. Ooh, I'm mad!"

Phoenix had never missed a class; not even for Caine. She pulled over to the espresso shop. She got one for now and two for the road. They sat outside in their spot, and Phoenix's anger softened when she saw Caine.

What the fuck? He gotta tracking device on us or what? Cahree couldn't stand being in his presence, and he knew it.

"Ladies?" Caine turned to Phoenix. "Yuh nah go to class, eh. Tink yuh too bright?" Phoenix scooted over and patted the empty space. She told Caine about Vina. He glared over at Cahree. "Why yuh nah call mi?" Cahree wasn't sure if he was talking to her or Phoenix. Cahree rolled her eyes. Phoenix began noticing the tension between them.

"Y'all, this ain't about you two. This is about me and that bitch! So cool it."

"Yuh nah chat to mi so. Answer de question. Yuh too bright, eh?"

Phoenix was shocked at his tone. She got up and walked away, ignoring Caine. "Come on, Cahree, let's get lunch."

Cahree smoothed her miniskirt and grinned at Caine. Puta! She was glad Phoenix picked up on his bullshit.

"I don't know who that niggah thinks he is, but he ain't hardly gonna be talking to me like that? Respect me or leave me alone."

"That's right, P! Now let's do lunch, but let's do it at home. I'll cook."

***

Felisha Bradshaw

Rajii, Kye, and Jamaira checked into their rooms after hitting 125th street. Jamaira had never been in an upscale hotel. She felt like a princess. She looked over at Rajii and smiled. Who knew my baby had it going on like this! I can't wait to see the room he got us.

THINK ABOUT IT

Chase called Lynx to see if he could take the trip to New York with him.

"No doubt, son! You think I'ma let you go alone? Something just don't seem right. Did Rajii say how he got out?"

Damn, this niggah is paranoid. "I'ma swing by and pick you up at the crack of dawn."

"Did you tell young Raj when you were coming? How you know Cutty didn't make him call, and it's not a setup? You did say that niggah wanted to kill you."

Maybe paranoia is a good thing.

"You right. I knew I called you for a reason. Let's leave at two in the morning, then. You know what to bring."

Chase hung up the phone and started executing a plan. Ever since all this shit went down, he's been losing his edge. Love will do it to you every time. Chase decided to drive his car because he had it equipped with a stash spot for his piece. If Cutty wanted war, war was what he'd get.

Chase sat on the edge of his sofa and thought about how he had it growing up. His father was always high. But whenever he did have a dime in his pocket, he gave Chase a nickel. Moms just didn't give a fuck. There was never anything to eat nor were his basic needs provided. The only reason the rent stayed paid and the heat and lights stayed on was because the social worker assigned to his family's case put his mom in every assistance program available. She thought she was helping to keep Chase in a decent home. Chase now wondered what his life would have been like if he had been adopted, like his brother. He could hear his mother saying: better be glad I got yo' ass back; don't worry 'bout his ass! But throughout his childhood, he always wondered if his brother was safe. Even though he'd never met him, he wondered every time he was in New York if one the faces he passed in the streets belonged to his brother. The thought left a knot in his stomach. He began feeling incomplete—the way he felt when he was a child. He wondered if Cutty knew about his brother, then dismissed the thought. He wasn't even sure how Cutty knew him. Just then, he remembered the number Lynx gave him.

Fuck it! It can't hurt. That man can't do shit he ain't already done. Chase retrieved the number then sat with his phone open, staring at the number.

His father didn't take long to answer. His father spoke loudly. Chase heard music in the background.

"Wha'um? Wha's yuh business?"

Chase took a few deep breaths before speaking. The sound of his father's voice brought back so many memories. Some good; most bad.

"This is Chase. I got this number from Cutty. It ain't about what I want. It's what you got to say."

"Ay, bwoy!" Chase's father yelled at someone in the background. "Cut it off! Dis mi pickney 'ere!" Silence came at his command. Chase wondered where he was. "Dese youts dunno nuttin. So, Chase, mi nevah tink mi 'ear from yuh. Yuh nuh muddah gone to a bettah place?"

Eyes on the Pryze

"Yeah, whatever. Listen, man, what did you want? How long have you been talking to Cutty?"

"Not long. So whey yuh deh? 'ow's tings? Long time mi nah 'ear yuh voice. Yuh no pickney nuh more, eh?"

"Cut the small talk. What do you want? I know this gotta be about money. Cutty had to tell you my position."

"Ay, bwoy! Mi still yuh faddah. Nuh disrespect mi, seen? Mi nevah ask yuh fi nuttin before. Yuh tink mi nuh bright? Yuh tink de business yuh did was secret? Mi knew from back den yuh was runnin dem tings feh de corner mon. Wha' yuh tek mi feh idiot? Yuh tink mi nevah know bout yuh stash box. Mi nevah teef from yuh den and mi was livin wrong den, too. Nevah!

"Mi gettah bad vibe bout dat day. Mi knew dat yuh was gonna meet trouble. So mi 'ad to keep an eye on mi bwoy. Mi 'ear tings back den. De streets dem haf eyes and ears. So when yuh run, mi send Cutty to look bout yuh. Mek sure yuh alright, seen?

"Mi 'ear yuh tinkin. Memories don't live like people do. Tinkin bout if yuh ever come short, but I tink yuh see dat yuh nevah. Maybe ovah, but nevah short. Mi know we was bad parents, but it was yuh muddah dat controlled de money. But when mi got a likkle, mi always mek sure yuh got a likkle, too, seen? Mi jus nevah chat bout it. Mi know yuh nah call feh dis, but yuh mus know mi always loved yuh. Mi ask Cutty to haf yuh call mi to tell yuh wha' mi learn from de streets. Wha' mi haffa say, yuh mus tek heed. ... Yuh dere, bwoy?"

"Yeah! Yeah, Pops, I'm here. So you saying Cutty knew I had the money from jump?"

"Listen, bwoy, pay attention. Mi know yuh nevah mek de buy feh de drugs dem. So mi figure yuh run wid de money. Dem Colombians dem whey 'ot like fyah. Deh bwoy dem lick shots pon, 'e nuh dead, son ... 'e nuh dead. Dey say 'e jus sleep longtime. Dey call it coma, right?"

"Pop, there's a lot of shit I need to know, and some shit I just want to get off my chest. I'll be in the city tomorrow. I'll check you or you can meet up with me. But I gotta go right now. Business calls."

"Chase, nuh sleep nuh one. When mi say nuh one, mi mean dat ... not even mi."

Before Chase could question his last statement, his father hung up. Chase had misjudged quite a few people. He seriously contemplated getting out of the game, and moving as far away from the street life as possible. *Maybe I'll open up some storefronts and chill. I can't live this lifestyle much longer. Shit ain't like it used to be; where everybody ate and everybody was content. Greed is a muthafuckah!*

Chase's pop never told him why he wanted him to call.

***

Chase called Rajii to see if he'd gotten settled.

"What's up, Raj? Everything a'ight?"

"Man, you just don't know. A bath can make things seem a whole lot better. Thanks for putting me up."

"You know that's right. Look, there's something I need for you to do. Write this address down and have the florist at the hotel send some flowers to Phoenix."

Since they had time now, Chase ran down the latest drama. The Phoenix shit bugged Rajii out, but the Vina and Phillie thing is what really hit him.

"So, you know I need you back on the team right after we split, a'ight?"

"Yeah, I know. The way Cutty was bugging. Saying some shit like you were walking in the shadow of death. Whatever that meant. All I'm saying, Chase, is keep your eyes open and your ears to the pavement. Sleep no one!"

"Rajii, you know I never sleep. Even when I'm napping, I ain't sleep. Feel me? Niggahs gonna catch the old Chase ... I don't believe shit till I see it, or pull Caesar till I need it. Believe that! One."

Chase strapped Lil Caes to his ankle and his ratchet knife on the other then made a quick stop at the bar. Venus had hit him on his Sidekick and left a message that could not be ignored.

"Yo, Venus, what's up?"

Venus finished serving her customers then pointed to the end of the bar for Chase to take a seat. She gave him the usual: cranberry, grapefruit, and orange juice.

"You and your virgin mixes. I hit you up cause I been keeping an eye on M.D. Everybody seems to like that niggah, but nobody knows him from the next man. They say he's fair on the business tip and he comes at you correct. What I wanted you to know is that he's been laying weight on a few dealers. New faces."

Chase sat back and watched M.D. at work. I think this niggah think we boys or something. Chase needed him to see that he rolled dolo. This niggah needs to know that it ain't the Jamaican in me he should fear—it's me—both sides. "Yo, my man, let me get at you!"

M.D. gulped down the rest of his Patron and took a seat next to Chase. Once M.D. sat, Chase rose and put his Timbs on the stool as if to tie them. He pulled his ratchet. Within seconds, it was at M.D.'s throat.

"We ain't boys. And just because I copped them bricks from you, don't mean you can do business in here! I told you before: shit don't go down if a niggah don't get down, you dig?" M.D. did all that he could do ... nod. "When I'ma get my candy?"

"Can I talk?"

"Shoot!"

"Your man changed the time and day, said he was going out of town for a sec."

Chase nodded. He hit Venus off then walked out. After Chase left the bar, M.D. walked over to Venus and handed her two bills.

BELIEVE IT OR NOT

After shopping, Blizz checked into a different hotel because of the tension between him and Kye. They made arrangements to meet up in the morning.

Rajii spent as much time with Jamaira as he could. They made love all evening. While they cuddled, he explained that he came for business; and no one needed to link her to him. He gave her five thousand dollars and told her to get her hair and nails done, and whatever she didn't get earlier.

"Too bad you didn't bring someone with you. Why don't you talk about any of your friends?"

"I see them when I can. We hit each other up on myspace to keep in touch. Maybe I'll call up one of my girls to meet me on 125th. You worrying about me? You need to hook Kye's ass up with somebody. Ever since his baby mother left, he ain't been seen with no chicks."

Rajii thought about it. "Right!"

They sat up for a little while longer then he said his goodbyes. She didn't mind so much because the damage he did in the bedroom made her fall asleep soon after he left.

Rajii returned to the room he and Kye shared. He found Kye in the living room, sprawled out, going through the selection of movie rentals.

Yeah, this niggah do need a new wifey. "I'm about to ask you to do something and you gotta be down. It's part of the plan." Kye sat up. "I need you to give me the business. I mean, really fuck me up."

"Nah, man, I can't do that."

"Come on, man, I told Chase Cutty was fucking me up."

Kye recalled the conversation. "Yeah, but you said the swelling went down."

Rajii grew frustrated. Bad enough he had to let Kye beat him in his face.

"But, how am I gonna have swelling with no bruises? What, you scared I could take your ass or something?"

Kye laughed. "You fucking with a thoroughbred." Kye playfully jumped on top of Rajii and jabbed him a few times. Rajii took this opportunity to make Kye hit him harder. Rajii slipped from underneath him and was now on top of him. He threw blow after blow in Kye's side. The harder Rajii hit him, the harder Kye hit back. Rajii placed his knee in Kye's chest and threw a blow to his jaw. Kye looked at Rajii to see if they were still playing, but couldn't read him.

"Blizz said you was a bitch ass niggah. I thought you had more game than that." Kye tried not to take it to heart, but the mere mention of Blizz set him off into darkness. To bring him farther into darkness, Rajii took it a step further. "Maybe if your ass wasn't such a bitch, Shotz would still be here."

Kye couldn't believe what his boy was saying. "Niggah, you don't know shit about me." Kye flipped Rajii on to the floor and started mutilating his ass. Blow after blow, Rajii regretted taking it there. Even blocking his face and curling up in a ball couldn't block the rage coming from Kye. When Kye saw Rajii bleed, he jumped back. He kicked over the floor lamp and started screaming. "Fuck Blizz! Fuck that bitch!" Rajii crawled to the couch. His face was pounding and his lip was slit from the last punch Kye threw.

"Damn, man! I wanted a few bruises. Yo, your ass is a beast." Rajii was out of breath. Kye paid no attention to Rajii. He paced back and forth with his gat out. Damn! I forgot that niggah was strapped. "Yo, Kye, man, cool down. I had to say that shit to get you to hit me. It ain't your fault about Shotz. They planned that. No matter what, it would have happened." Kye drew his gun on Rajii. "Yo, man, it's me, Rajii. Come on, man, snap out of it. It's me."

Kye came out of darkness. "Raj, did I hurt you, man? I'm sorry, man."

"Yo, man, you need to settle that guilt shit within yourself. It's eating you up. After this is done and over, we gonna get you some help."

Rajii went to the bathroom mirror and was shocked. He looked like a few niggahs got at him. He ran the hot water and placed the rag over his face to take away the throbbing. He cleaned up the blood that dripped from his lip. It was difficult for him to get any kind of sleep. I know to never go head up with his ass.

***

Blizz sat up in his room going over the instructions Caine gave him. He hadn't visited New York in a long time. Ever since he did his bid on Rikers Island with Caine, he knew things were going to change for him. No more selling packs for PC. He thought back to when Caine was his cellmate. A group of Colombians approached Caine, looking for beef. He'd been on the island a few days because he didn't make bail. Blizz was about to get out after serving a five-year bid. Six slick-headed dudes ran up in their cell. Blizz had been skimming off their product, so he thought they were coming for him. But they grabbed Caine, held a knife to his face then, suddenly, put him down and left. It freaked both of them out; even if neither said so.

Later that evening, before lockdown, the *HCIC came back with a bodyguard and apologized for the mix-up. That's how Caine learned the rumors of him having an identical twin brother were true. Not having a scar on his cheeck saved Caine from being killed that day. But he wasn't in the clear. The HCIC made Caine an offer: help him or die. He sweetened the deal with one hundred thousand in cash and a smooth connect to their raw. The Colombians then poisoned Caine's mind against Chase. They led him to believe that Chase had a life to be envied, and that Chase had always known of his whereabouts, but didn't care about him. Caine has hated his identical twin ever since.

Even after Caine blew up, that hatred ate at him. He wouldn't rest until he destroyed Chase; the brother who turned his back on him. And the HCIC wouldn't rest until he avenged his son. Yet, neither the HCIC nor Caine wanted Chase dead. They wanted something much worse. They wanted Chase to suffer.

---

* *Head Colombian In Charge*

MIRROR, MIRROR, ON THE WALL

Phillie called Chase to let him know he needed to pick up Vina, and that she would stay behind; so Chase and Vina would have the time they needed with Phoenix without any distractions.

Lynx was checking into Hotel Chelsea when he saw a familiar face in the lounge.

"Young Raj. What up, kid?" Even though Rajii's hair was cut, it didn't stop Lynx from recognizing him. He never forgot a face. To him, everything else about a person was irrelevant ... extras. "Damn! Man, your shit is fucked up."

"Where's Chase? I didn't know you were coming." He gave Lynx the 357 handshake. Lynx then tapped him on his shoulder. Rajii winced at his touch.

"Damn! Who banged you up like that? What the fuck happened to you?"

"That niggah, Cutty, man. He's straight-up bugging. He had my ass tied up in some warehouse and shit."

Kye walked up to them and introduced himself. The way Lynx kept questioning Rajii on the sly, like he didn't believe his story, made Kye suspicious of him. Kye changed the subject by asking Rajii if they were still on for brunch.

"We can all meet up right here after I pay for these rooms and get settled in. Maybe Chase will be here by the time we come back."

Lynx agreed. He wanted to keep a close eye on Rajii and his friend. "Give me a few minutes and I'll be back down."

After Lynx walked off, Rajii filled Kye in on what to say if Lynx asked how he got out of the warehouse. Kye then enlightened Rajii about the ill-feeling he had about Lynx.

"Yo, that niggah is straight trying to read you. Let's get this shit popping, so we can get rid of his ass. One slip, and he'll know this was a set up. He's got to go!" Rajii and Kye made their story airtight.

"Remember, nothing more, nothing less."

Lynx settled in and called Chase.

"Yo, man, something just ain't adding up." Chase skipped over Lynx's paranoia and asked how Rajii was doing? "His face is fucked up, and I barely touched his ass, but he looked like he was about to fall over. So maybe the ass whooping was true, but there's something in his eyes that ain't telling the whole truth. We about to do a late breakfast, so handle what you need to do and I'll hit you up when we're done. Then you can see for yourself what I'm talking about. One."

Lynx freshened up and met Rajii and Kye back in the lobby.

Chase and Vina were on their way to see Phoenix.

"I'm telling you, Chase, don't get your hopes up. She didn't look like she wanted to hear shit."

Chase took in everything Vina told him during the ride. When they reached Bleecker Street, Chase parked at the corner. They looked at each other, got out the truck, and took deep breaths.

Eyes on the Pryze

"It's now or never."

"Go ahead, my nerves are a mess," she shoved Chase up the steps. They stood at the door for what seemed like hours before Chase got up the nerve to ring the bell. Chase checked his watch then turned to Vina.

"Who's at the door, boo?" asked Phoenix.

Phoenix couldn't believe what she was witnessing. She looked at Caine then her and Chase's eyes met. "What the fuck?"

"What's going on, Phoenix? Who is this?"

Phoenix looked back at Caine. She couldn't move, let alone answer. Cahree came to the door to see what the commotion was all about. "Ay Dios mio!"

Chase wanted answers. He stepped into the doorway and reached for Phoenix. Caine stepped in front of him. Chase swung at Caine. Not because Caine blocked him from Phoenix, but because he wanted to make sure he wasn't seeing things; make sure the image before him, his image, was real. The punch landed in Caine's midsection. Caine's first reaction was to draw his gun. "Nuh mek nuh move!"

Vina screamed, "No! Don't!" She grabbed Chase's arm. "Chase, this isn't right! None of this is right."

Cahree stood silently. Her eyes fixed on Chase. She debated whether now was the time to speak up. Phoenix ran upstairs.

"Phoenix whattah gwan?" Chase pulled his arm from Vina's grasp. Caine took the safety off his gun. Vina grabbed Chase again.

"Fuck this!" Chase walked down the steps then turned back and pointed to Caine. "Yuh nuh bloodclot scare mi, 'ear? Tink mi nuh big mon, eh? Vina, mi gone." Chase walked off. Never once did he look back. Vina yelled after him, but he still didn't looked back.

"Carmen, please let me talk to her. Please?" Caine stepped aside, allowing Vina to pass through. Cahree closed the door. "Where is she?" Cahree pointed to the stairway.

Phoenix lay across the bed staring at the ceiling.

"What the fuck is going on, Phoenix? Who is that?" Phoenix said nothing. "He pulls a fucking gun on Chase and you just walk away? What's going on? Answer me." Vina grabbed Phoenix and shook her. "Do you hear me, Phoenix?" Vina had no choice but to slap the shit out of Phoenix.

Phoenix sat up, her eyes filled with tears. "His name is Caine. I met him—"

"I don't care where you met him. Couldn't you see he's identical to Chase? What the fuck is wrong with you?"

"I kept seeing him everywhere. But I couldn't catch up with him. When I did, I thought he was Chase. But then he was so different. I was trying so hard to erase Chase from my mind, I feel in love with Caine."

"I don't care how bad you tried to forget Chase. Look at him. He looks just like him. Why didn't you say anything to Chase? He didn't deserve that."

Phoenix laughed maniacally. Vina backed away.

"He deserves what? How the fuck you gonna come to my house talking about what he deserves? You fucked him and now you're the keeper of his feelings? Fuck you and what he deserves. I didn't deserve what you two did to me. Deserve?"

Eyes on the Pryze

"Look! I told you at the school. It wasn't what you thought. Ever since you stopped speaking to me, this has been heavy on my heart! I couldn't figure out for the life of me why you stopped speaking to me. Then when Chase said you weren't speaking to him either, we figured it out."

Phoenix stood up. "It took you a while to figure out what? That I saw y'all? He carried you in the house and took hours before he came out, tugging on his pants and shit. Bitch, please."

Neither of them noticed Cahree standing in the doorway.

"Listen, Phoenix, you're like my sister. I would never do anything to hurt you." Phoenix looked away. Vina stood in front of her, turned her face to her. "You should know the same goes for Chase. He's been going crazy!"

Tears fell from Phoenix eyes. "Then why, V? Why did you do it?"

Vina asked Phoenix to sit back on the bed. The horrors of that night replayed in her head. She cried. "Phoenix, I was raped the night before you saw that. I was gang raped. I don't even know who did it. When Chase came that night, I thought he was the one who raped me. I swung at him with a bat and lost my balance. He caught me and carried me in the house. I was a mess."

Phoenix's mouth dropped. All this...all this for nothing. She held Vina in her arms and they rocked back and forth and cried. Cahree had tears in her eyes when she walked away. Vina then went on to explain that night in full detail. She even shared her feeling about Phillie. Everything was out in the open. Cahree then returned and came into the room.

"He's gone, P. Caine mumbled some shit about getting something, or maybe he said somebody, and he left."

Vina stood. "Chase! We gotta find him and explain." Vina ran out of the house calling his name with Cahree and P in tow.

***

Chase couldn't believe what he'd just witnessed. Everything that happened since Cutty kidnapped Rajii replayed over and over again in his head. Then he remembered the look in the man's eyes who answered the door. He wasn't shocked to see me. He wasn't shocked to see that he looked like me ... me like him. "What was Phoenix doing with him?" Chase had to sort this out, but knew he couldn't do it alone. He had no one to call but Lynx. "Yo! Whe' dey? ... A'ight me soon come." Chase, so distraught, hailed a cab to meet Lynx and Rajii.

***

Meanwhile, Caine called Blizz to fill him in on everything that went down. "Mek it 'appen!"

Blizz called Jamaira to cancel their brunch date.

***

Before their orders were served, Lynx received a call on his cell and excused himself from the table. Kye saw a familiar face come into the restaurant. He tapped Rajii on the leg.

Eyes on the Pryze

"Damn! Beef! I knew we should've left Blizz back in the Port. We played ourselves." Kye turned around to check for a getaway then reached into his pants leg and released his piece from his ankle and sat it on his lap.

"Who?" Rajii search the restaurant.

"That niggah with the dreads. That's Caine."

Rajii looked up from sipping his glass of OJ. "What? You mean Chase?"

Kye was completely confused. "No, man, that's Blizz's boss. That's Caine."

Chase reached the table and Kye held his hand on his gun. Chase hugged Rajii. Rajii jerked in pain.

"Shit ain't swollen no more, but that shit still hurts."

Chase nodded at Kye. "Thanks, man, for helping my lil niggah out. What's ya name?"

Kye stared at Chase's scar on the side of his face. "Kye ... you?" Kye still hadn't taken his eyes off the scar on Chase's face.

"Chase. My name is Chase. Where's Lynx? I got a jewel I wanna drop on y'all. None of y'all gonna believe this shit when I tell it."

Kye couldn't believe his eyes. Lynx walked over to the table and greeted Chase with the 357 shake.

"What's good, man? You take care of that?"

Chase took a deep breath. "I was just telling Raj and his man here I got some shit to drop that's gonna fuck y'all heads up! I went to talk to my girl with Vina and, when I knocked on the door, guess who the fuck answered?" Chase asked around the table for the answer.

Lynx leaned forward and took the first shot. "Another niggah?"

Chase's laugh was wicked. "Negative." He pointed to Rajii.

"A naked bitch?"

Lynx couldn't help but laugh. "Niggah, Cutty had your ass locked the fuck up too long. You got pussy on the brain."

Chase shook his head. "Wrong again." He then pointed to Kye. Kye was laughing at Lynx's statement.

"I ain't even gonna front. I was hoping you were gonna say some freaky shit, too."

Chase shook his head again. He then looked around the restaurant and shouted, "Anybody else wanna fucking guess?"

The patrons in the restaurant stared over towards their table. Lynx was eager to know why his boy was straight tripping. "Man, who?"

Chase let out that wicked laugh again.

Yo, this niggah is bugging. Kye put his hand back in his lap.

"Me. I answered the fucking door. Me, fucking me. I was staring at me. It was like some Matrix shit. The door opened and it was fucking me standing on the other side. You believe that shit?"

Lynx and Rajii were beginning to worry about their friend. The stress from the business and matters of the heart had taken their toll on Chase.

"No, for real, man. Stop fucking with us."

Chase twisted up his lip and gave Lynx a look that said 'man, I ain't playing'.

Eyes on the Pryze

Rajii sat back. "Man, how the fuck you answer the door and you was doing the knocking?" Chase's eyes told no lie. Rajii and Lynx knew him all too well. "Explain that shit."

Chase explained what went down at Phoenix's place. Kye wasn't the least bit surprised. After he broke that shit down, Kye knew he was referring to Caine. Rajii and Lynx remained skeptical.

"See, I told you, man. That's Caine." Kye leaned in closer. "Caine is Blizz's boss. He runs the Dough Boys. When I saw you come in the restaurant, I was like, what the fuck? Cause I got beef with them niggahs for some shit they did to my boy. They had my man killed. When I saw you, I told Rajii that you were Caine. But he said, nah, Chase not Caine. Lynx, man, check this shit." Kye pointed to his lap.

Lynx stood as Kye leaned back to reveal his piece. "Yo! This niggah ain't playing. He got Molly sitting on his lap."

Chase asked Kye everything he wanted to know about Caine. Kye filled his head with truth, but spiced things up a bit, too.

"Yeah, that niggah will do what he needs to do to get his. His boy, Blizz, sends his soldiers to do all the executions."

"How you come to be such an expert on the Dough Boys?" asked Lynx. "Seems like you know too much ... and if you was down with them, then how you know Raj like that?"

Kye knew what Lynx was trying to do. They were so much a like, so he gave Lynx what he wanted. "I don't need y'all to like me. Feel me? What I do is what I do. But since you grilling me like that, check it. I used to be a major player on the Dough Boys' payroll. I was one of the first Blizz recruited. He's blood, fam, but when that niggah killed my boy, making me believe it was on some drive-by shit, he gets no more love from me.

"Fam is Raj here. We ride to die for each other. I trust him with it all. Feel me? I got to know this cat through my cuz, Jamaira. He's been kicking it with her for a while. She's like my little sis and he treats her right, so we got mad cool. When this niggah called me, I chewed his ass out cause he just up and disappeared on my cuz. But then he told me what was what, so I came through. It took a lot to get him through that tight ass window, but my man here is a soldier and we here. Trust!

"If you ask me, I think Cutty was playing both sides. Because the warehouse I got him from was the same one we used to pick up bricks from the connect. So call me a snake or switch, but I want Blizz's ass to catch a dirt nap. Fam or not. He's got to get it. So when y'all ready to do this, I'm down."

Lynx looked at Kye with new respect. "I feel you, man. Fam is in the streets for me, too. That bloodline shit is for the birds! When I wasn't eating like this, my fam said fuck me. So to me, Chase and Rajii here and most of 357 are fam to me. Even though you ain't 357, welcome to the fam!"

Lynx gave dap to Kye and lowered his wall of suspicion. Not entirely, cause he learned from the Cutty shit that everybody can't get one hundred percent trust. Everybody raised their glasses.

"Welcome to the fam."

It was official. They were all on the same page; with the same agenda. Blizz and Caine had to be dealt with.

Eyes on the Pryze

***

Vina, Phoenix, and Cahree just missed Chase getting into a cab.

"Damn!" Vina was pissed Chase walked off with the keys. They hailed a cab then Vina pulled out her cell phone. "Where you at? ... Oh yeah, I talked to Phoenix and told her everything. ... What you mean, so what? She wants to talk to you. ... I know, but ... Well anyway, I need the keys to the car. Is that your brother? ... Nah, he left after you did. ... I don't know. Chase, be safe." Vina closed the phone. She could see Phoenix knew what Chase said about her, but he was right; so there was nothing else to say. For the rest of the ride, each dwelled on her own thoughts.

Chase wanted so much to see Phoenix; to hold her again, but she had crossed the line. The only person who could answer with certainty whether Caine was his brother was his father. Chase was just about to get the answers he needed when Lynx got a text message on his cell.

"Yo, what the fuck?" He passed the Sidekick to Chase.

You're beat!

Chase checked the phone number the text came from. M.D.'s number showed up. "Yow, mi nuh play wit de fuckery. Beat? Mi beat?"

Lynx grabbed the cell from Chase and called M.D. Voice mail picked up. The recording told Lynx that he was beat for his shit. At the end of the message, M.D. said, "Thanks, and you can keep the bricks." Lynx could hear his laughter; making Lynx's anger skyrocket.

"Yo! There's gonna be a lot of slow singing and flower bringing."

Kye thought, A man after my own heart.

Chase felt so stressed, he held off calling his pops. Instead, he called Vina.

"Yo! Mi gotta mek a run. De desk man will 'ave de keys. Hotel Chelsea. Stay dere and mi soon call yuh back."

Vina redirected the cab driver to drop them at Hotel Chelsea.

When they returned to the hotel, Rajii asked if he should bring the bags with him and checkout.

"Nah, man, we ain't got time for that. Kye where's your ride?"

Kye looked at Rajii and Rajii handed over the keys. Lynx thought it was strange that Rajii had the keys, but he dismissed the thought. There were more important things to think about. Kye handed the keys to the doorman and, in no time, the doorman pulled up in the Cadillac truck.

"I see you doing big boy things." Lynx was impressed.

On the way back to Bridgeport, they discussed how they were going to get Blizz and Caine in the same place to take them both out before they figured out what was what.

GUESS WHAT?

Vina called Phillie to tell her what went down on Bleecker Street.

"Get the fuck outta here. Is Chase a'ight?"

"Phoenix and I are cool again. As for Chase...well, he's okay, just not with Phoenix. I think that guy's his twin." Vina said to Phillie then turned to Phoenix. "Remember when Chase sat with us down in Newfield Park, when we called ourselves running away because we had to go to Laurelton Hall, and Chase kept us company?"

"Yeah, the only reason we went home is because Chase told us that he wished he had parents that cared about him."

"He said he had a brother, but DCF took him and the mom only got him back. Remember?"

"Yeah, but he never said it was a twin."

"Maybe he didn't know. I remember him saying his mother wouldn't talk about him."

Cahree sat back in silence. No need for her to say anything, they were on the right track.

"So this niggah, Caine, is his twin?" Phillie asked. "Do they look just alike? Phoenix was fucking him and you gonna tell me that she didn't know."

Vina whispered, "worse. But this Caine guy doesn't have the scar. Everything. It's like looking in the mirror."

Phillie wondered if Phoenix knew and just didn't care or if there was more to the situation. She worried for Vina's safety.

"Where y'all headed now? Where's Chase?"

"Chase took off with the keys, so I left the truck at Phoenix's. We're on our way to Hotel Chelsea to pick up the keys at the front desk. Chase told me he's on his way back to Bridgeport. He said something about taking care of some business."

"Hotel Chelsea? What was he doing there?"

"I don't know, but that's what he said. He told me he'd call me later. I guess the room is paid for."

"Alright. I'm with Lex. We're waiting for Genisis to finish her intern rounds at St. Lukes. We'll meet you in the lobby."

"Okay. I love you. Bye."

Phoenix turned and smiled at Vina. Although she didn't know all the details of how they hooked up, she saw a familiar look in Vina's eyes. The same look she always had when she was with Chase; now Caine. "Y'all serious, huh?"

Vina blushed. "She's my other half. I feel so complete with her. And the sex is off the chain! Girl be having my toes curling and tears in my eyes. She works that thang."

Cahree wanted to know more. She recalled the strap-on thingamajig that the guy in the toy store showed her. She knew she could please herself, but just think if she had another woman to do it. The thought rushed through her mind. Whew!

"Ooh, girl, j'all done did it. I saw a girl-on-girl movie and they were using that strap-on thing. That's when I started understanding what they got out of it."

Vina laughed. It was more to her than penetration, but she decided to let Cahree have her fun. "I know that's right! Carmen, you doing some research, huh? Let me find out your a closet freak."

"My girl here has been holding that thang tight. She don't know nothing 'bout that."

"That's what joo know! I got me a new Denzel. Battery operated." Cahree stuck out her tongue. "So there!"

Phoenix gasped. "When? How did you get it? You didn't tell me."

"Ah ha! Wouldn't joo like to know? I even had an orgasm. A whole lotta orgasms." Cahree stuck her tongue out at P again.

The cab driver turned around, drooling. They looked at each other and burst into laughter.

"Yeah, he would like to know, too!"

Embarrassed by Vina's comment, the driver turned around and didn't look at them again until he pulled up to the hotel.

"Thirteen dollars, ladies."

They giggled in unison stepping out the taxi.

WHAT TIME IS IT?

Jamaira was enjoying her day with her girls: Baby, Cassidee, Adjonae, Tequa, Tynesha, Tianna, and Mequa. They made up the Dymez 'R' Us crew. She treated them all to a fresh pair of whites and similar jean suits.

Baby watched Jamaira peel off hundred dollar bill after hundred dollar bill. "Girl, you done hit it big. What Blizz got to say about this?"

Jamaira filled her girls in on what's been going on lately. Usually, she heard about their drama and adventures. But this time she did the talking and they did the listening.

"Bout time you put his mean ass in his place." Cassidee always had something negative to say.

"So when we gonna meet this Rajii?" asked Adjonae, genuinely happy for Jamaira.

"Soon, y'all, real soon."

Mentioning Rajii made Jamaira realize he hadn't called her all day. She hit him up as soon as she entered the dressing room.

"Hey, bay! Where you at?"

"On the highway, ma. I'll have to fill you in on what's what later."

"What? See, Rajii, I thought no secrets. I know you and Kye are up to something. Don't make me worry about y'all."

Eyes on the Pryze

Rajii smiled. He loved his ride or die chick. "Listen, ma, finish up shopping with your girls and I'll call you tonight if I'm coming through."

Jamaira knew that meant he couldn't say much more, so she left it at that. She'd cuss him out later. "Okay. I'm bringing my girls back to the hotel. That a'ight?"

"Just stay outta Kye's room; you know he probably got some shit around that he don't want fucked with, but yeah, that's straight. I'll call you when we can talk more."

Jamaira whispered, "I love you." All Rajii said was 'me, too'. Niggahs hate to show they're whipped in front of their boys.

FRIENDS? HOW MANY OF US HAVE THEM?

Vina, Phoenix, and Cahree entered the hotel lobby. All heads turned. The young ladies were all beautiful in their own way.

"May I help you ladies?" The front desk clerk stared at Phoenix's breasts as he spoke to Vina.

"Excuse me, Boo-Boo, but I'm over here." Vina held his chin and turned it in her direction. He was just as pleased to look at Vina. Her lightly glossed full lips did something for him. "Yes, you can be of service. Chase Pryze left his room and car keys for us."

The front desk clerk could only wish he was as lucky. "Are you all his wives?" He couldn't believe he said that out loud. "Excuse me, I'm very sorry, Are you his wife?"

Cahree giggled at the man fumbling with his words. Just to make his day, Vina answered him.

"Yes, we are. Excuse me, yes, I am." Her answer both intrigued and embarrassed him. He retrieved the keys and the attached note. "Thank you."

Before they walked away, each blew him a kiss. His chocolate skin flushed. They giggled and headed to the elevator.

"Did you see that fool. He was practically drooling." Vina unfolded the note and read it then handed it over to Phoenix.

Phoenix stood frozen as a tear ran down her face.

Just when I thought my life was coming to an end, I saw you. I love you, Phoenix. Nothing has changed.

Love, Lies, and Loneliness,

Chase.

"Vina, I fucked up! I really fucked up." Phoenix didn't know what to do. She loved Chase and had been loving him for years. They grew together, knew each other. But then there was Caine—she loved him, too. She wondered what Chase meant by love, lies, and loneliness. She understood he loved her, but what were the lies? And who felt the loneliness? She was so confused. She wished she'd listened to Vina when she tried to talk to her back in Bridgeport. I really fucked up! Phoenix held the note to her heart.

"What are joo feeling, P? Joo have to listen to jor heart. That's where jor answers lie." Cahree prayed that Phoenix chose Chase.

Vina began to like Cahree. At first, she thought she was trying to take her place; but she could see she had Phoenix's best interests at heart.

"That's right, Phoenix, listen to your heart. Remember all the times you had with Chase. The good and the bad. Think about the things you shared with him that you never shared with anyone else. I understand that Caine makes you feel brand new cause Phillie does that for me, but are you willing to let go everything you and Chase were to each other for something new? I know you said Caine makes you feel like woman, but, baby, no man can do that. They can only respect the woman that you already are."

Cahree smiled at Vina. "Damn, girl, joo making me wanna cry." Cahree turned to Phoenix. "She's right, though."

Phoenix had a lot to think about. They entered the suite and plopped down on the sofa, waiting for Chase's call.

THOUGHT THEN PROCESS

Side Effect had its usual sized crowd for the first time this evening. Venus prepared drinks and collected tips from customers. She saw Lynx and Chase enter with Rajii and Kye in tow. They all looked about business.

I thought that young one dipped with the cash flow. Venus caught wind of all the rumors. It was part of her profession to have a listening ear. She didn't think she'd put herself in harm's way because the paper she was getting from both sides had more weight than her worries. Lynx motioned for Venus to come to the end of the bar.

"Give me a shot of Patron," he looked over his shoulder and asked if they were straight.

Kye tried to raise his hand to signal he wanted a drink, but Rajii gave him a look of disapproval.

"That's all your crazy ass need. You need to stay on point."

"Yeah, you're right. Thanks, man, but I'm straight."

Venus walked off to make Lynx's drink. She returned and slid his drink to him. "What's up, Chase?" Chase's eyes spoke for him. Tonight he was not to be fucked with.

Lynx finished up his shot. "Look, Venus, cut the bullshit. Where's M.D.?"

Venus told Lynx what she was paid to say. "He was in here earlier. He told me to look out for you. Oh yeah, he said to tell you that you can keep the bricks and you know the rest ... whatever that means. I haven't seen him since, and tonight's a busy night. He's usually posted up at the other end of the bar." Venus pointed to the empty seat by the door. "Ain't nobody seen him. A few of his outside customers have been looking for him, too."

Chase called over the female who was up in M.D.'s face the last time he was in the bar. "Shorty, call M.D. for me."

Shorty told Chase she'd been texting and calling him all day and all his calls were going straight to voice mail. Lynx grabbed her phone and called M.D. This time it didn't go to his voice mail, the phone was cut-off. Lynx gave her phone back, hit her off with a twenty dollar bill, and looked at Chase.

"What you wanna do?"

Chase slammed his fist on the bar. "Whatta bloodclot! Dis bwoy nuh play mi? Cha!" Chase hissed his teeth.

Rajii and Kye stepped back. Rajii always knew to back off when Chase spoke in his father's native tongue.

"Yo, he got us both. You know I'm usually paranoid about trusting people, but he even had me hyped. I thought things were going to be straight. That was loot. Muthafuckahs is having a field day with your cash. Fuck these greedy bitch ass niggahs."

Chase looked over at young Raj. "Yow, yuh still got dem bags, right?"

Words refused to come out of Rajii's mouth, so he nodded instead. He was curious to know where this was going. He finally spoke once he saw Chase's eyebrows rest.

"Back at the hotel. What's up?"

"So, can I set up the buy?" asked Lynx.

"I know you want to give him the business. This way, we all can get what we want. I know that niggah set us up."

Kye loved where this was headed. He smiled. "Like catching two birds with one stone. I'm wit' it. What you got in mind?"

"Make sure you tell Blizz that, in order for this to go down, Lynx has to do business with the bossman only. Set it up for tomorrow night." Chase turned to Rajii. "Do you think we can catch Cutty slipping? I wanna check out this warehouse. We're gonna take his ass out, and get the rest of my shit. When this niggah, Caine, shows up with the product, we can take him and Blizz out. Long as I get that niggah and half of the cash and all of the product, it's all good."

Lynx was definitely impressed. "Now that's the Chase I know and love!"

Chase addressed the three men in his corner. "After this shit is over, we're gonna have to rearrange how this crew operates. Kye, if you want in, you got it. You're like fam now, but we can make it official. Think about it. I know now who'll ride to die for me and I want you three on top of things. Let's head back to the city. Get some rest. Kye handle the business. I got some shit of my own to take care of. This time, there's no exception to the rule. Those who ain't with me, are against me. Anyone against me, is the enemy."

It was done.

They left the bar after tipping Venus. They jumped in the Caddy truck, and Kye pumped Biggie all the way there.

kick in the door
waving the 44

"That's my shit!" Lynx was a huge Notorious B.I.G fan. He got hyped on the next song. It was familiar to them all. They sang out in unison.

it's the ones that smoke blunts witcha, see your picture

Lynx rolled a blunt.

now they wanna grab guns and come and gitcha

They rapped along with Biggie until the song ended. Each focused on his own thoughts the remainder of the ride.

Kye rolled down the window, remembering how he reacted to Haze.

Rajii felt sorry for his girl. Damn! But a niggah's got to go!

Chase hated how shit had to be. He finally meets his brother, now he has to kill him. Phoenix, why? He thought about Phoenix laying up with his blood.

All Lynx thought about was sparking up another blunt. He bounced his head as he listened to "Warning". He laughed to himself. How ironic that song played at that time. In no time, they pulled up at Hotel Chelsea. Rajii and Kye had their own agenda.

"We'll be back. We're gonna get some grub and case out the warehouse. Shit has to be waterproof," Rajii said.

Lynx nodded as he and Chase exited the truck. "Check for the best way to get up outta there without being seen. We'll handle the rest from this end."

Rajii pulled off.

"Yo, what the fuck? How we gonna do this? We need some duffels like the ones Cutty had. We gotta fill 'em up and set up a scene at the warehouse like we told them. Damn!"

Rajii and Kye had some work to do. Rajii hoped he would have time to see Jamaira. He needed to see her. He didn't know how shit was going to end up. It might be their last time.

HIM OR ME? CHOOSE!

Phoenix slept on one end of the couch. Cahree slept on the other. Vina laid out on the floor as she talked to Phillie on the phone. Phillie never made it to the hotel.

"You know I do." Vina twirled a lock of her wavy hair. ..."I can't do that. ... So what they're sleep. ... Girl, you're so nasty!" Vina and Phillie tried to catch up on the time they spent apart. They truly fell in love in New York. You know the saying: New York is for Lovers.

The door slowly opened and in walked Chase. He had no idea that Vina, Phoenix, and Cahree were still there.

"Shh." Vina pointed to Phoenix and Cahree. His love, the beauty to his beast, looked like an angel sleeping. He stood over her and watched her sleep. Lynx nodded at Vina. She waved. Lynx headed to his room connected off of the living room area.

Chase couldn't believe he finally had a chance to talk to Phoenix and she was sound asleep. He lightly sat on the arm of the couch just above her head. He whispered to Vina.

"Boo-Boo, I'll call you back. Chase is here. ... No, she's sleep. ... Okay. ... I love you, too. See you tomorrow. ... I know. Early. Bye."

Chase yearned to run his hands through her hair. He, instead, leaned over to smell her scent. She wore a different fragrance from her favorite Dolce & Gabanna. This reminded Chase that she may have changed. Though the scent she now wore was light, he longed to smell her favorite fragrance.

"Give me the heads up?"

Vina started to fill him in, but Phoenix awoke. She saw the man she betrayed, and still loved. The triangle she was caught up in made it unbearable to look him directly in his eyes.

"Hey beautiful!" Phoenix lowered her head. "It's alright." Chase got on his knees and rested his arms on the end of the couch. "Talk to me, ma. I need to know that we are still one." Phoenix dropped her face into her hands. She covered her eyes to avoid seeing the pain in his. "I wish you knew me better. I thought you did. I would never hurt you like that."

"I tried to fight it. I battled with my decision for a very long time. But then when I called you and you lied about where you were, it was like you confirmed what I didn't want to believe. Why did you lie?" Phoenix's eyes became watery. No matter how much she tried to fight back the tears, she just couldn't.

"I gave Vina my word. My word is bond. I wish I could turn back time to do things differently, but I can't.

"There were so many mistakes made and so many 'I wishes' and 'I wouldas'. It made forgiving you or not forgiving you a hard decision to make. I want you to know no matter what you decide, I will always love you; and I will wait for you to learn that I'm the only man for you."

Chase rose and walked into his bedroom. His bed felt twice as empty as it ever felt before. After Cahree heard their conversation, it was hard to hate him. She wanted to see the beast in him, but she didn't. He had so much love for Phoenix; there just couldn't be any room in his heart for a killer or a thief.

"I think he means every word he said, Phoenix."

Vina agreed. "Chase has always loved Phoenix. When we were younger, he was that kid who didn't say much. But when Phoenix came around, he wanted her to know he existed. The girls loved that he was quiet and the fact that he was getting dough, but he never showed them any type of attention. He always did for Phoenix. She knows who will love her always. Don't you?" Vina didn't need her to answer her because she knew it was so. She prayed it was so.

Phoenix rose and walked towards Chase's room. He undressed as she knocked on the door.

"Who?"

"Me. Can I come in?"

"You should know the door is always open for you, Phoenix."

A faint smile fell over her lips. "I think we need to talk." Chase sat on the bed and patted the space beside him. "I want you to know that when I met Caine, I thought he was you ... but then the scar." She ran the tips of her fingers over Chase's scar. It sent chills through his body. She noticed what it was doing to him, so she stopped. "Then we started talking. All I saw then was the difference in you two. It sort of blocked out him looking so much like you."

"So what you saying, Phoenix? You love this niggah?"

"I didn't know I would. I just was trying so hard to move on."

Eyes on the Pryze

Chase jumped up. "You love that niggah? It took you a year to even say those words to me, and you up and love another muthafuckah just like that! Choose, Phoenix. I won't be played with. Make a choice. Now! It's either him or me."

"I can't!" She stood and left.

Chase slammed the door behind her. *Oh, that niggah has got to go!*

"What happened, P?" Cahree stood when she heard the door slam.

Phoenix ran passed them. "I gotta go!"

Cahree said goodbye to Vina and followed Phoenix out the hotel room. Vina ran into the hall to give Cahree her cell phone number.

"I'll call joo."

Vina knew things didn't go as she'd wished or as Chase wanted. She went into the room to find out what happened and to console him.

TO STAGE A KIDNAPPING

It took forever for Kye and Rajii to find an abandoned warehouse that they could access. It took even longer to find a store that sold duffel bags identical to the ones Cutty always used to do pickups and drops.

"This is it." Rajii called Kye to him. Rajii was on his knees peeking into the perfect place to stage the kidnapping.

Kye returned to the truck to get the props: an old swivel desk chair, rope, and the duffel bags. They used the base of the chair to break the window then crawled inside one after the other, and immediately began staging the scene.

Kye positioned the chair near a dilapidated desk found in the middle of the area. Rajii nibbled at parts of the rope. He noticed an old trash can beside the desk. He pissed in the trash can and told Kye to do the same, and to do so until they left.

"Good thinking!"

They scoped out how large the area was and the closest exit of the two. They could either use the door or pull the rope to open the garage door. Rajii unlocked the door to see where it led. Perfect! The door led to the street. A smooth getaway. By the door were stacks of empty boxes.

"If Chase stands here, he got a clean shot at anybody who comes in." Rajii made a mental note to tell Chase.

Eyes on the Pryze

Kye hid in the mist of the boxes then stacked them to about Chase's height. "Now no one will even know he's there. What if they make us come clean of all our guns? What we gonna do, then? I don't know too many niggahs that let you stay strapped when a buy this big is going down."

Rajii was glad he had Nina and her little sister on him. He knew Kye was always strapped. Kye and Rajii looked for a stash spot for their guns.

"The desk. Make sure you're leaning on the desk when shit goes down. You want to be able to access it at any time." Rajii searched the desk and found just what he was looking for. He taped little Nina under the desk. "What about you?" Rajii knew Kye never felt safe without a piece on him or nearby.

"I'll put mine in the duffel bag. When he asks to see the money I'll get it, then." Kye sat his piece on top of all the paper stuffing in the bag. Kye and Rajii went over everything again then left the same way they came. This time, they stacked crates by the window so they could get out easier. Once they reached the truck, Rajii jumped in the driver's seat and combed the outside of the warehouse.

"Now, let's set up the buy."

Kye called Blizz and cringed at the sound of Blizz's voice. After convincing Blizz everything was kosher between them and that this was about business, Blizz called Caine to okay the buy. He knew something didn't seem right, but every time he thought about the money he would make in PC, the thought was quickly dismissed.

Blizz never told Caine that Kye set up the buy because he didn't want him to back out. Once Caine gave him the okay, he called Kye back.

"It's a go. Where and when you wanna meet?" Kye gave the address to the old warehouse in the Meat District and set up the buy in two days, at midnight. "A'ight! Kye, don't try no bullshit. You know how Caine rolls."

"This ain't about you and me. This is about the grind. Once I get my share for hooking this shit up, I'm out for good. Deal?"

Blizz didn't give a fuck about what Kye wanted to do, long as his ass stayed as far away from him as possible. "No doubt!" Then I can serve that bitch ass Rajii since the beef is squashed with Kye. This should be easy as pie.

Kye hung up. He couldn't wait to tell Rajii the deal was on.

TENDER LOVE

Rajii stopped by Jamaira's room to spend some time with her. He knew she was upset when he last spoke with her. By the time he reached her door, the guilt of having to kill Blizz resurfaced. He prayed she wouldn't notice. Rajii tapped on the door. An unfamiliar face answered.

"Hmm, you must be Rajii."

Rajii wasn't sure how she knew his name. He checked the room number. Then he remembered Jamaira saying she was bringing her crew back to the room. "Yeah, I'm Raj, and you are?"

The girl in the baggy pajama pants and wife beater said, "Adjonae, but you can call me Adj. Everybody else does."

Rajii flashed his pearly whites. "Okay, Adj, where's my baby?"

She stepped aside and told him Jamaira was in the bathroom. Adj took it upon herself to introduce Rajii to the rest of the crew. They said their hellos and he immediately walked to the bathroom.

Damn, it's tight in here. I gotta get her girls a room.

He stepped over shopping bags and girl type shit and knocked on the door.

"Dang, y'all, can I get some privacy? I'm taking a dump." The girls laughed. If only she knew. Rajii opened the door. Jamaira was so embarrassed. "Raj!"

Rajii smiled. "Damn, baby, you smell like you're pushing out a dead body." He stepped in and shut the door behind him.

"Get out!"

"We gonna live together and I'm bound to know that you shit just like everybody else."

He had a point.

"I didn't think you were coming. Now I got company. You leaving, huh?"

"The way it smells in here, you damn straight. I gotta get some air." He kissed her on the forehead and walked out.

"Rajii!"

Rajii handed the girls a wad of bills and told them he wanted to spend time with Jamaira. It was more than enough for them to get a double and have room service money leftover.

"Ooh, we like you." Cassidee smiled. "Come on, y'all, let's bounce. Tell Jam we'll see her in the morning."

They gathered their things and left.

Rajii heard Jamaira turn on the shower. He placed candles around the room. "This is Room 229, could you send up some OJ, fresh fruit, whipped cream, and melted chocolate?"

The order was brought up before Jamaira finished showering. Rajii removed his clothes and walked in the bathroom just as she turned off the water. He slid open the glass doors and stepped in.

"Aw, Raj. I just knew you left me. Where my girls at?"

"Got them a room. I needed to be with you."

Eyes on the Pryze

He turned the water temperature to hot. The heat of the water against his back relaxed him. Jamaira lathered up the washcloth and began bathing her man from head to toe. When she reached his manhood, she held the base of it and gently glided her hands up and down. It drove Rajii wild. Although she already bathed, he returned the favor. He rubbed her clit until it was slippery and hard. He backed her up against the wall and raised her in his arms. When he finally inserted her, she moaned out in ecstasy. Rajii stroked her slowly. She backed up on his shaft and rotated her hips faster and faster. He didn't want things to end, so he pulled out of her and turned her around. Her ass was perfectly shaped. She placed her hands against the wall as if he was about to search her, and slightly bent over. She had never let him enter her this way before. He was gentle with her. Tonight she would show him just how much she loved him. She spread her legs and touched the floor.

Damn!

Rajii rode her ass till he burst inside her. She stood and held Rajii until he stopped shivering. Rajii carried her to bed for round two. Awakening with her in his arms was something he planned to do for the rest of his life.

Rajii called Kye to see if he was up for breakfast. To his surprise, Kye told him he had been up for a while, and Chase and Lynx were on their way up to the room.

"A'ight. I'm gonna hop in the shower and we'll be there."

Kye was thrown by the whole we thing. "You bringing Jamaira?" Rajii sighed. "You think she just gonna let me leave? Just tell them niggahs not to talk about business at breakfast."

Jamaira woke. "Who was that? I know you ain't about to bounce?"

Rajii grabbed her and tickled her stomach. "I would never make love to you and then bounce in the morning. Them days for me are over. Now get up and let's go eat. Your girls said to be ready."

Jam tapped him across the head playfully. "Yeah, I am hungry. Now, who was that?"

Rajii laughed. Jamaira was always on point. There was no misleading her.

"That was Kye. I called to wake him up. Maybe you can hook him up with one of your girls."

Kye, Dymez 'R' Us, Rajii, Jamaira, Lynx, Vina, and Chase met in the lobby.

"Everybody here?" Lynx asked sarcastically. He wanted to get down to business.

Rajii introduced Jamaira to Chase. "This is my girl, Jamaira. She was shocked. She didn't know Rajii and Kye settled their beef. Then Chase turned to her. No scar. Rajii picked up on Jamaira's expression. He quickly introduced her to Lynx.

"Nice to meet you, ma!"

"These knuckleheads over here are her girls."

After the introductions, they sat and had breakfast. Not much was said and that was fine with Rajii. The slightest slip up and Kye and Rajii were dead men.

"Let's meet back in the lobby about six. We got shit to handle." Chase was agitated. He hadn't gotten a wink of sleep since his quarrel with Phoenix.

Rajii planned to spend the day with Jam, her crew, and Kye. Cassidee was hot on Kye's trail. Rajii was beginning to wonder about his boy. Kye hadn't noticed what was so obvious.

"What's up with you, Kye? Cassidee has been trying to push up on you all morning."

Kye checked out Cassidee. She smiled at him. Kye leaned in towards Rajii. "I'm more of the quiet type. Sorry. Plus, I still have love for my baby mother."

Rajii gave up. He rejoined Jamaira to let Cassidee down easy.

"I wasn't sweating him, anyway. He ain't even on my level."

Yeah, uh huh!

After lunch, it was getting close to that time. Rajii tried to make up an excuse. "I thought Lynx said six. It ain't even 4 o'clock yet," Jamaira said.

"We gotta check out, gas up and everything. Plus, them niggahs ain't gonna ride my shit all over New York. I want to get a rental car, so you and the girls can ride back in the Caddy."

Jamaira pouted, but knew it was a no-win situation. But she wasn't going to settle for that sorry reason.

"Raj, I know y'all up to some shit. I wanna know what's going on. When I saw that guy you call Chase, I thought it was Blizz's boss, Caine. What's up with that? And he didn't look too happy. And who was that chick with them? She seemed to be staring at you all morning. What's up with that, huh?"

Rajii noticed Vina had stared at him, too. He hoped she couldn't ID him as one of her assailants. His whole love story would be blown right out the water. He was glad she didn't say much to him. But that look in her eye ... she was trying to figure shit out.

"Huh?"

"You heard me! Who is that girl?"

"I know you peeped that Chase shit. He just told us the other morning about that niggah, Caine. I think it's his twin. He's the one behind setting Chase up to lose all his dough."

"What does that mean, Rajii? You and Kye ain't been telling me much lately, so I don't really know shit. I ain't even seen Blizz the whole time we been here. I called his hotel room a few times and talked to him, but he always seemed caught up in some shit with Caine."

Rajii explained what he could without telling her about the warehouse. He touched on Phoenix running to New York because she thought her best friend was sleeping with her man; and she ended up dating Caine, claiming not to know they were twins.

"I don't even know half of what's going on. Kye and I have been filled in piece by piece. The shit is crazy, right?"

Jamaira wasn't going for that. How could that girl not know? She knew there was more to the story. Rajii always ended his stories with a question when he was lying, just to see if he had you believing him.

"Whatever, Raj. I'm telling you if I find out you're leaving something out, you better be ready for a fight." Rajii laughed and threw his fists in the air and started jabbing at her. She couldn't resist his silliness. "Yeah, whatever. You think I didn't notice the bruises on you?" Her eyes saddened. She wished he would confide in her.

"Oh yeah, that came from Kye." Jamaira knew they were up to something. She threw her hands on her hips. Before she could fly off the handle, Rajii explained. "I had to let him do it. I told Chase that Cutty had me locked up in a warehouse and was fucking me up. I was tired of running from Chase. I wanted to get my life back on track, so we could be free to go and do whatever. You feel me? Don't you want that for us?" That was only part of the truth. He left out the part about the plan to kill her brother.

Jamaira began to understand ... sort of. "Oh ... okay." The only thing that bothered her was Rajii ended his explanation with two questions.

Rajii and Jamaira caught up with Kye and her friends. Kye finally loosened up around her friends. They were window shopping. The girls tried to get Kye to come out of the young boy look.

"That would look good on you, Kye. Leave that jersey shit for them busters that ain't on your level."

Kye liked the style they were pushing at him. "Yeah! Those shoes are nice. I could see that on me." *I'm gonna need a suit anyway to wear to Blizz's funeral.* "Yeah! Maybe this weekend we can take these girls out to the 40/40 Club and show them how ballers really get down!"

Rajii prayed they'd make it till then.

They went into the store and tried on a few suits and shoes.

"He's so full of himself." Jamaira referred to Rajii flaunting himself in front of each mirror he came upon. Kye looked like a whole new person. "Damn! My cuz is fine! Do that walk, cuz!"

Kye strutted back and forth for the Dymez. Cassidee wasn't having it. She was going to get this man to play on her team. Kye and Rajii brought a few suits and headed back to the hotel.

Kye gave Jamaira instructions to the location of his safe, bank books, and a letter to his lawyer then he hugged and kissed his little cousin.

Rajii kissed Jamaira like it would be his last. "I love you, ma."

She felt a sadness in that kiss. "Rajii, tell me I'll see you back in Bridgeport. Promise me that, and I'll chill out."

Rajii held her face up to his. "I promise. Now tell me you love me."

Jamaira still worried. "I love you, Raj."

Rajii handed the keys over to Jamaira and a envelope that held a letter he wrote the night before; expressing to her how he felt and apologizing for keeping secrets from her. It explained what they were about to do and gave the address of the warehouse and everyone involved. It also had all the numbers to his family and a combination to the safe. Rajii previously had Kye take an insurance policy out on him; making Jamaira his beneficiary.

"Don't open this until you get back to Bridgeport. Give me your word."

Jamaira looked at Rajii and a tear fell from her eye. "You promised you were coming back. You promised."

Rajii kissed the tear from her cheek. "And I'll make good on it. Now promise me."

Jamaira mumbled between sobs, "I promise."

She knew it was a promise she wouldn't keep.

I JUST CAN'T...STAY AWAY

Phoenix sat on the living room sofa. She hadn't seen Caine since yesterday. She didn't understand why he stayed away because she hadn't chosen Chase. If anything, things seemed like she wanted to be with him, not Chase.

"Mami, what happened back there? Why joo come out crying?"

"I want Chase because my heart really doesn't know anything else. I keep asking myself was I attracted to Caine because of the way he looks. Or because of the different way he treated me? I don't know what to do. Caine says he loves me and wants to be with me for the long run. I want to believe him. But there's something about him that makes me question that. I know Chase says what he means and nothing less. How could he forgive me after what I've done?"

"Joo would give up the years that joo and Chase had to be with someone joo are unsure of? How joo know the only reason joo even liked Caine was because joo were on the rebound? Rebounds never last. Would joo be willing to give all that up? He will forgive joo and can because his love is strong."

Phoenix knew what Chase wanted from her. The time had come to know what Caine wanted.

"I need to talk to you. Can you come here as soon as possible?" Phoenix thought she heard him hiss his teeth. Caine acted as if Phoenix asked him to perform a miracle.

"Mi soon come."

Phoenix couldn't believe he hung up. Just like that.

Caine pulled up and told Phoenix and Cahree to come with him to make a quick run. "We cyan talk aftah mi handle dis business." He only took the women with him so he wouldn't look suspicious in the Meat District this time of night. Women always served as a decoy in his line of business.

SIX MILLION WAYS TO DIE...CHOOSE ONE

Kye pulled up to the front of the hotel with the rental car and beeped the horn for Rajii, Chase, and Lynx to come out. Kye was so hyped, he set the mood for the rest of them.

"So tell me what y'all come up with then I'll hit y'all with what I came up with."

Chase still dwelled on his conversation with Phoenix. She just can't ... after all we been through. Cha!

"I think Chase should lay low. If they see him, they'll know we're out for blood." Lynx said. "Ain't this it, Raj?" Rajii nodded. "Let's take a ride around the warehouse to make sure we can get ghost when we need to. Shit needs to be planned from the inside. We're gonna come outta this on top."

Rajii had Kye drive one time around the warehouse just to be on the safe side. When they pulled up to the front of the warehouse, they saw the door open. Kye turned off the headlights and slowly pulled up to the loading area. They exited the car, leaving the doors slightly ajar. They crept up to the door and slid inside with their armor out. Once they got inside, they split up. Rajii checked on little Nina. Straight!

Lynx yelled out, "One!"

The others yelled out the same, letting one another know their area was clear of Cutty. Kye went back to the car to get the duffels from the trunk. When he reached inside the warehouse, he strategically placed large flashlights so they would have clear sight of one another. They met up in the middle of the warehouse.

"What the fuck is that smell?" Chase walked dead into the garbage pail of piss. "Damn, niggah, he had you pissing in the garbage?"

Rajii nodded. "Check this, I just taped my little bitch, Nina, under the desk. I'ma post up right here."

Chase saw the chair and rope that Kye and Rajii had staged.

"Damn, man, Cutty be watching too much TV. He did this shit up!"

Kye was now standing by the chair. He dropped the duffel bags at his feet. "I guess you can sit in the chair Lynx and I'ma stand right here."

Lynx liked the plan. "What about my man? Where should he post up?"

Rajii took Chase by the boxes and told him that he should wait in the cut, just in case they bring in someone else. Lynx thought they planned this a little too well. But then thought, he was in this bitch, so I guess he would know where everything is.

"What we gonna do if they ask us to throw out our pieces?" Kye asked; not wanting them to think he had all the answers.

"Yo, I ain't giving up my shit. That right there is a no-no. Maybe I'll tape my second piece under the chair. Yo, Raj, throw me that tape." Lynx taped his gun under the chair.

Shit was set in play.

***

Jamaira gave Vina a ride back to Lex's place. She had ill feelings about the letter she'd tucked in the sun visor.

"What's up, Jam? Your mind ain't been with us ever since we left the hotel."

Jamaira told the girls what Rajii told her to do with the letter. Vina was concerned for Chase.

"Read it! Maybe it has something to do with Chase, too. He did take that run with them, too, right?"

Jamaira said she didn't want to break her promise to Rajii. Vina then told her what giving your word could stir up. "He said you, not me. I'll read it. That way you won't go back on your word." Jamaira agreed and handed the letter to Vina, sitting in the passenger seat. Vina read the letter from Rajii. "Look, he even has his safe combination and..." Vina sifted through the attached papers, "...and insurance policies? What the fuck are they about to do?"

Jamaira told her girls that she wasn't about to lose her man to no fucking beef. "I'm gonna ride or die for mines. Y'all with me?" The Dymez were down for whatever. "You, Vina?"

Vina made it unanimous. "We need my girl and her crew." Vina called Phillie, gave her the 411, and the address to the warehouse. "Bring your camcorder. We might need it." She tried to call Phoenix, but got her voice mail. Damn!

Jamaira turned the truck around and headed for the Meat District. Baby expressed concern about them not having any protection. Adj reached into her handbag and pulled out a .25. Everyone looked at her.

"Shit, this is New York!"

Cassidee looked over at Mequa and they said in unison, "We should've known."

Meanwhile, in the heart of the Village, Cahree sat in the backseat of Caine's utility truck as Phoenix sat in the passenger seat, staring out of the window. Caine hadn't said one word to her since they hopped in the truck.

What's up with him? Why is he being so cold? Phoenix could feel the distance between them. "Where are we going?"

Cahree remained silent. She knew the area all too well. Her father did a lot of business out this way. Caine ignored Phoenix's question. He flipped open his phone and dialed Blizz.

"Whey ya deh? Okay, mi soon pull up. Five minutes. Nuh mek no move till mi touchdown, seen? Yuh call Papi? ... Good. 'im give yuh de stuff? ... Good. Likkle more."

Cahree's suspicions were on point. She sat back and wondered what else Caine was up to. They pulled up to the warehouse.

Caine pointed in Phoenix's face. "Wait 'ere. Nuh come outta de cyar." He slammed the door before Phoenix could reply. Caine stood at a Chrysler 300S and spoke in to the window. Shortly thereafter, Blizz stepped out of the passenger seat, and the car pulled off. Caine then took two large bags from Blizz and walked towards the warehouse.

Cahree noticed a truck and a car pulled up behind them and dimmed their headlights. She questioned Phoenix to see if they were on the same page.

Eyes on the Pryze

"Is Caine in the drug business? Cause this is where my father's people either dump bodies or make drops."

"I dunno. Looks like that's what's going down. Who's that behind us?" Phoenix turned around.

RIDE OR DIE CHICK: It's on and Poppin

Phillie and Lex got out of the car to speak to Vina.

"We're gonna go around to find a window, so we can get this shit on tape. Get in Lex's car; just in case we need to make a run for it. If I say go then leave, pull off. This ain't a game. I'm serious."

Cahree turned to her side, so she could see out the back window and talk to Phoenix at the same time.

"It's two guys. But I can't see who they're talking to."

Vina stepped out the truck to get behind the wheel.

"Ay Dios mio!"

"What? What?"

Cahree put the pieces of the puzzle together.

Vina ... and that must be the dyke that I thought was sort of cute, and that other one. That must mean Chase is in there. Oh no! Cahree didn't know what to tell Phoenix.

Phoenix turned around to look out the back window. She caught a glimpse of Vina. "What? What the fuck? Is that Vina? What is she doing out here in the middle of nowhere?"

Cahree shrugged.

Phillie squatted at the rear of the warehouse. The broken window gave her a clear view. Phillie checked the battery to make sure everything was up and ready.

Eyes on the Pryze

Caine walked into the warehouse with the bags of coke. Blizz pulled up the rear.

Look at this bitch. I bet he thinks he'll live to spend this dough we got. Kye had a sinister grin on his face.

Lynx, on the other hand, sat in the swivel chair with his legs cocked open and his elbows resting on his knees. "We gonna do this or what?"

Caine handed the bags to Blizz. "Mek de mon see a brick."

Blizz, never taking his eyes off Kye, reached in the bag and retrieved a brick and handed it to Lynx. Lynx handed the brick to Kye. Kye pulled out car keys and slit the bag open. He then rubbed the coke on his gums and waited for the freeze.

"It's straight! So what we talking?"

"Fifteen five. As yuh buy more, mi mek de price go down."

Lynx nodded and tapped Kye to go ahead with the buy. This was also the signal to get shit popping. Blizz noticed Kye grilling him.

"Yo! I don't like the way this niggah keeps eying me." Blizz spoke over his shoulder to Caine. "You know what, guns at your feet. Why we gotta get all personal with shit, Kye?" Blizz shook his head. "That's bad for business, man. It makes business bad. Let's see the money, too."

Rajii placed his gun on the floor in front of him. Kye did the same. Lynx bent and placed his gun at his feet.

"Now put your feet on your pieces." They all obliged. "Cool. Now the money."

Before Kye reached in the bag, he wanted to confront Caine about Shotz.

"Yo, Caine, we always been cool with each other. I wanna know something; cause no telling when we'll see each other again."

"Shoot, bwoy."

"I wanna know why you gave the okay to kill my boy. We always stacked major paper for you."

Blizz interjected. "Man, fuck that old shit! Shotz was riding your hustle. You should be glad we took that bitch ass niggah out." Blizz had gained some balls in front of Caine.

"Kye, dat's inna de past. Plus, Shotz was a botty bwoy!"

When Kye heard them bash his boy's memory, he flipped out.

"Whatever, man! Let's just do this."

Rajii sat on the desk. His trigger finger itching. He knew his boy couldn't take much more. Kye picked up the bag and reached inside. Before Blizz realized Kye drew his piece, the first shot hit Blizz in his stomach; the second hit him in his chest. Blizz fell to the ground. Lynx took the gun from under the chair and pushed the chair at Caine. Rajii grabbed Little Nina from under the desk and jumped behind it.

"That's for Shotz, muthafuckah!"

Blizz tried to reach for his gun and Kye sent him into darkness. One to the head.

Caine let out a shot that skinned Kye in the upper body. Kye fell to the floor.

"Kye!" Rajii came out blazing aimlessly. He reached Kye's body as Lynx covered him. Rajii dragged Kye behind the desk. "Yo, man, you a'ight?"

Kye nodded. "Yeah, man, I'm a'ight it hit me in the shoulder. If I died today, it would be okay knowing I didn't let Blizz live after taking it to my boy. That was for you, Shotz!" Kye noticed Rajii was bleeding. "Yo, man, you hit."

Caine ran by the door and tried to make a getaway. Chase popped out from behind the stacked boxes. "I told you I'd see you again."

Phoenix heard the shots ring out and ran into the warehouse. The door pushed open and Caine grabbed Phoenix.

"Caine!" Phoenix then realized he wasn't trying to save her, but used her as armor.

"Mek de shot! Mi know yuh nuh wanna hurt your gal. Come on, bloodclot!"

"Let her go! This is between you and me! Let her go!" Chase backed up. "I'll put my gun down if you just let her go."

Lynx aimed the gun for Caine's head. "Chase, don't do it. I can take him. Don't do it. Either you shoot that niggah or I will."

"This is my beef now, Lynx. Let me do this. If you miss, he'll kill her. I can't have that!"

Phoenix struggled to get away from Caine.

"Look, gal, yuh wan dead?" Caine tightened his grip on Phoenix. She noticed the ratchet knife in his waistband.

"Fuck that! Your beef is my beef." Lynx was just about to pull the trigger when a gunshot hit him in his lower back. He fell to the ground.

Rajii and Kye looked where the shot came from. On the far side of the warehouse, they saw a glare from a gun then legs passed by the small window. They saw the shooter's shadow ... then he was gone.

"I didn't even notice that window before. Who the fuck was that? Where did Phoenix come from?" Rajii whispered to Kye. Neither had a clear shot of Caine.

"You're in a no-win situation here. If I put the gun down and you shoot me, my boy, Rajii, and his man is gonna fill you with Teflon. So just let her go, and we'll let you go."

Caine laughed. "Ya wrong star. See de bullet dat lick your bwoy? Mi 'ave back up, seen? If de bwoy dem lick shot, my bwoy on de outside will lick shot. So put de gun down. Now!"

Caine never felt the knife being lifted from his waist. Phoenix slit him from his ear to his mouth. When he screamed, she flinched and dropped the knife. Not before giving Caine a scar identical to that of Chase. The pain caused him to release Phoenix. "Yuh dead now, seen!" Caine reached for Phoenix. Chase let off shots. One bullet hit Caine in the chest. The other hit his midsection. He stumbled back and grabbed Phoenix. "Mi a soldier, seen?" Caine lifted his shirt, revealing a bulletproof vest to Chase. Caine dragged Phoenix to the door.

Jamaira couldn't stand not knowing if Rajii and Kye were alright. She took Adj's gun, exited the truck, and ran to the door; where she saw Caine dragging Phoenix.

Chase yelled at Caine to let Phoenix go once more.

"Shoot him, Chase! Just shoot him!"

Caine yelled, "Finish dis, gunman!"

Just when the man on the outside was about to shoot, Lex hit him over the head with a steel pipe.

Eyes on the Pryze

Caine thought he was in the clear, so he aimed the gun at Chase and fired. Chase fell into the stacked boxes. One shot towards the head; one to the chest. The third shot missed him.

"Now feh yuh." Caine put the gun to Phoenix's temple. Jamaira shot him from behind. He fell instantly.

Jamaira screamed, "Rajii, where are you!" Rajii had fainted from the sight of his blood. Lynx didn't have the strength to answer her. He slipped in and out of consciousness.

"They're behind the desk. One of 'em is shot!" Phoenix said, then ran over to Chase.

His words were faint. "I still love you. Now and forever." Chase used all his strength to reach in his pocket. "Call my father. Let him know." A glob of blood oozed from his mouth; his eyes shut. Phoenix gripped Chase's hand and screamed.

Cahree entered the warehouse. It was bloodbath. She saw Phoenix leaning over a body.

"He's gone, Cahree, he's gone!"

Cahree told P she'd called the police and that they needed to leave.

When Jamaira saw Rajii laid out, she screamed, too. Kye came to and said, "He's a'ight. Get the bags from Caine. Get us outta here, cuz."

They heard sirens in the distance.

Lex, Phillie, and the Dymez came running in. They got the three wounded men, the drugs, and money out the warehouse and into the cars and truck. Phoenix crouched over Chase.

"Mami, we have to go. We have to go!" Vina pulled her friend off Chase with Cahree's help.

"Wait! I think he's breathing."

Vina looked over at Chase's body and knew there was no hope. "Come on!"

When they passed Caine's body, he was as dead as Chase. Cahree spit on him. "Puta!"

Police and ambulances arrived on the scene, as well as news reporters. It was Detective Mathew's first case on his new job as NYPD's head homicide detective. Detective Mathews walked into the warehouse and knew this was a drug deal gone bad.

"Check these bodies and see if anyone's still alive. I need answers."

The paramedics checked the bodies.

"We have a live one, but I doubt he'll make it." They put him on a stretcher and placed him in an ambulance.

"Detective Mathews, we found this outside one of the windows." an officer showed the detective a cell phone and empty shells.

"Send those to ballistics. I want fingerprints lifted. Hopefully, we can trace them to our shooter." Detective Mathews left the scene leaving the bodies behind for the coroner.

Miles away, Jamaira told Adj to stop the truck.

"They need medical attention."

Lynx bled all over the backseat, and Kye continued losing blood. Rajii's bullet wound was only a graze. The cars following them stopped. Lex got out seeing what the problem was.

"What's up? Why you pull over?"

Adj pointed to Jamaira in the back of the truck.

"Lynx and Kye are losing a lot of blood. They might die if we don't get them help." Jamaira held Kye in her arms and held Rajii's hand.

Lex had to think quick. She knew they couldn't take them to the hospital. "Follow me!"

Everyone followed Lex back to her garage apartment. Once they arrived at her place, Lex jumped out the car and pulled open the garage door. They pulled the cars and trucks inside. Lex woke Genisis from a sound sleep. The moment she saw their injuries, Genisis immediately went to work on Lynx, Kye, and Rajii.

Phillie tried to calm Vina down. Cahree held P's head in her lap, gently massaging her scalp. Phoenix still held the piece of paper in her hands.

"What's this?"

Phoenix sat up to use the telephone. The least she could do was carry out his last wish.

"Uh, is this Mr. Pryze?" Phoenix cleared her throat.

"Ya, mon, dis 'im."

"This is Chase's, Chase's girlfriend. He told me to call you ... he's dead."

He rubbed the lump on the back of his head, "I know ... I know."

Felisha Bradshaw resides in Bridgeport, Connecticut and is currently working on the sequel to "Eyes on the Pryze", called, 69 Degrees coming fall 2010 She is a graduate of Housatonic Community College, holding an Associate's Degree in General Studies and is enrolled in Ashford University where she will graduate June 2010 with a bachelor's degree in Psychology and a minor in Sociology

LaVergne, TN USA
06 January 2011
211398LV00003B/34/P